SINK THE *PRINCE OF WALES*

Malaya, November 1941
Major Nairns, on an intelligence patrol on the borders of Malaya and Siam, stumbles on a Japanese seaplane reconnaissance base. With international unrest looming, Nairns' instincts tell him they are up to no good. Further surveillance reveals the Japanese plan to eliminate any British ship which might interfere with their proposed landing on the outbreak of war. There is only one such ship at risk – the brand-new 'unsinkable' HMS *Prince of Wales*. In a desperate race against time, Nairns sets out to warn the authorities, pursued by the feared Colonel Moto and his secret police...

SINK THE *PRINCE OF WALES*

SINK THE
PRINCE OF WALES

by

Duncan Harding

Magna Large Print Books
Long Preston, North Yorkshire,
BD23 4ND, England.

British Library Cataloguing in Publication Data.

Harding, Duncan
    Sink the *Prince of Wales*.
    A catalogue record of this book is
    available from the British Library

    ISBN   0-7505-1536-8

First published in Great Britain by Severn House Publishers Ltd., 1999

Copyright © 1998 by Duncan Harding

Cover illustration by arrangement with Severn House Publishers Ltd.

The moral right of the author has been asserted

Published in Large Print 2000 by arrangement with Severn House
Publishers Ltd.

Magna Large Print is an imprint of Library Magna Books Ltd.

Printed and bound in Great Britain by
T.J. (International) Ltd., Cornwall, PL28 8RW

I still remember the chill sense of calamity which was caused by the loss of these two ships. It was worse than calamity. It was calamity that had the premonition of further calamity... For the first time we had an inkling of the true balance of this Pacific war. We saw before us, still vaguely perhaps, that long dark tunnel through which we should have to pass before we emerged in the sunlight on the far side.

Ian Morrison, War Correspondent, 1941

As I turned over and twisted in bed the full horror of the news sank in upon me. There were no British or American ships in the Indian Ocean or the Pacific except the American survivors of Pearl Harbour, who were hastening back to California. Over this vast expanse of water, Japan was supreme and we everywhere were weak and naked.

Winston Churchill, 11 December 1941

Prelude to Disaster

So we beat on, boats against the current, borne back ceaselessly into the past...

Scott Fitzgerald, The Great Gatsby

The tropical sun cut his eyes like the blade of a sharp knife. Major Nairs narrowed his gaze against the glare. He peered at the wavering ball through the gap in the jungle canopy and felt almost sick. The heat and the humidity were almost unbearable.

Next to him 'Nobby' Clark, crouching with the rest of the dark little men from his Malay Scouts, sighed and whispered, 'Cor ferk a duck, what I wouldn't give fer a pint of wallop back home.'

'Put a sock in it,' Nairs hissed at his old batman, now his second-in-command, 'They can't be far away now.'

Nobby pulled a face. 'Ferking Nips – can't ferking see ... can't fcrking hear.'

11

'Wouldn't bank on it,' the major said and took his compass bearing, working out the remainder of his course as he did so. Whatever the wizened-faced little cockney, who had been with him since Peronne in 1918, thought to the contrary, he knew the Japs were good soldiers. They had to be. Hadn't they conquered half of Asia over the last decade? And now they were on the very edge of the British Empire itself. The question was: were they going to attack Britain, now that she had virtually lost the War to the damned Huns in the West?

A sharp crack. The hollow boom of a rifle shot, muffled by the jungle, echoed back and forth to their front where the border lay with supposedly neutral Siam. Next to him Nobby started. The dark-faced Scouts, their features lathered in sweat as if they had been greased looked at each other in alarm.

Nairs acted quickly. They were good little blokes, intensely loyal to him, but they were flighty, easily panicked by the unknown. Swiftly he said in his fluent Malay, 'No need to fear. Nipponese shooting game for food.' He made the Malay gesture of shovelling in rice with his hand to his mouth.

They smiled warily, appeased. Nobby Clark looked at him, unappeased. Nairs knew what that look signified. 'Don't say it,' he hissed urgently. 'All right, move your *derrière*. Move!'

Hastily the little patrol moved and slid back into the tangle of the jungle, steadily following the big tough officer with his weary, cynical face, who looked as if he had seen everything – and then some. Seconds later they had disappeared into the dripping tropical greenery, as if they had never been there...

'Nairs,' Colonel Hathaway, the CO, had said, carefully sucking at his cold pipe as if he were giving the matter some considerable thought. 'I'm afraid it's got to be you.'

Outside, the plantation was settling down for the night. On the veranda, the half-naked Indian punkah wallah tugged the rope back and forth with his big toe wearily. Inside the punkah stirred the stiflingly hot air and everyone prayed silently for the coolness of the evening soon to come.

'I know,' the old CO, another veteran of the trenches, continued, 'you've got your rubber and your – er – other commitments here.' With the wet stem of his old briar he indicated Susi, nice, round and plump, sweating prettily as she prepared 'egg

13

banjoes' for the two them.

Naturally she didn't need to do the cooking as the 'tuan's lady'. She had servants enough, for the London-based Vulcan Malay Rubber Company was very generous with its allowances to its planters, even if they broke the unwritten rule and took an Eurasian mistress like Susi. But as the CO had observed earlier on, 'Can't trust any bugger these days, Nairs'. She'd agreed and dismissed the house wallahs immediately – even his old bearer.

'I see, sir,' Nairs had said and had waited. He had learned long ago when he had been a teenage subaltern with the Fusiliers back in France never to jump the gun. You got yourself killed – *swiftly* – like that.

'But, Nairs,' the CO had continued, 'you're an old hand. You know the land, the peoples, speak their lingoes like – er–' he had flashed a quick glance at Susi frying the eggs on the spirit cooker, 'a native. You've been out here, so the people in the club say, since the bloody year dot.' He had paused and taken a sip from his warm scotch.

Nairs smiled. His hard faced cracked into the grimace which was a smile for him, as he thought of the lonely life he had led here ever since he came here in 1919 to forget

14

the slaughter and shambles of the trenches. The old CO was right. What had it all been about – the nightly drinking sessions, the occasional discreet sex with one of the girls smuggled in by his bearer from the workers' compound, the annual leave to the fleshpots of Singapore. Not much of an existence. And all the while, every waking moment dominated by that bloody white fluid running out of countless acres of rubber trees which kept the West running.

'So *I* need.' He had paused awkwardly with his pipe, as if suddenly embarrassed. *'Your country needs you.'*

'To do what, sir?' he asked coldly, as if he had not heard that rather crude appeal to his patriotism.

'This. You know as I do that the Nips are on our border. Unofficially they haven't taken over Siam to the north of here, but thanks to those damned treacherous Frogs in Indo-China, they have.' He let his words sink in, while at the stove Susi pushed back a lock of her jet-black hair, smiled at him fleetingly and finished off the second banjo.

'And, sir?'

'I don't think you need a crystal ball, Nairs, to know why. They're preparing for the invasion of Malaya. All the signs are there. Intelligence tells us they're readying their fleet off Indo-China. Troop trains are bringing down their infantry and tanks by the battalion from China every day and they're flooding Malaya with their agents.'

Nairs looked grim suddenly, as he thought over swiftly the old CO's words. He was right about the Malays. Strange natives had been appearing regularly in the compound of late. There had been lots of whispering and significant looks when he had appeared by chance. Then the tame, broken-down, Indian imported labour had become sullen and resentful, as if it was his fault they had been forced to leave their native villages and journey hundreds of miles to earn a few annas and a bowl of rice in this remote plantation.

'I take your point, sir,' Nairs broke the heavy, brooding silence, as Susi bowed and placed the hot banjoes in front of them with her usual silent grace. As she turned he caught a glimpse of her dark belly under the sari and felt an almost physical shock. Did he deserve a body like that – an old cracked-up planter, whose liver had gone and who would probably snuff it before he was fifty? His type of old Malay hand always did.

Hathaway grinned carefully, trying not to

display his ugly yellow false teeth. He knew the feeling. But the 'memsahib' hadn't indulged him in that 'nonsense', as she described it, for a very long time indeed.

'Now Nairs, I want you to take a patrol of Scouts right up to the frontier – to the east – and see what you can see of the Jap. I'm sure he's there–' He paused suddenly and cocked his greying head to one side.

Nairs opened his mouth to speak, but Hathaway held up his hand for silence. At the little cooker Susi stood abruptly rigid, the fork still held in her dainty brown hand in a stupid sort of a way. Then Nairs heard it – the soft drone of a plane, going round and round steadily, as if it were looking for something – and even as he heard the plane, he told himself with a sudden feeling of shock, *there isn't a British airfield within three hundred miles of where we are sitting at this very moment!*

That had been forty-eight hours before. Now, as the little patrol pushed on, hacking its way through the primeval jungle, breath coming in harsh, hectic gasps, skinny bodies, brown and white, lathered in hot sweat, Nairs experienced that same feeling that he had done when he had first heard the strange plane. It was that of doubt and uncertainty, yet at the same time an awareness that all was not well with the world: the knowledge that something dramatic and startling would happen soon.

Time passed leadenly. There was no sound save the harsh gasp of their own breathing. Even the birds and the normal persistent chatter of the monkeys had ceased. The very air seemed heavy with tense expectancy. Next to Nairs, the undersized cockney in his absurd, overlong shorts, with the heavy rifle slung over his skinny shoulders, croaked, 'Fuck this for a game o' soldiers, sir, if you'll forgive my French–'

Nairs nodded he would.

'But, as Paddy would say, "sell the pig muvver and buy me out." I've had a bellyful. There's something very peculiar–'

He never finished the complaint. For suddenly, startlingly, the thick jungle ceased. It was as if someone had drawn a line and had hacked away all the vegetation along the length of it. For abruptly the trees had vanished. In their place was a patch of bare yellow turf, with beyond it the glittering sparkle of the Gulf of Siam, motionless, turgid, a leaden grey mirror in the tropical heat.

But it wasn't the sudden sighting of the

18

sea which surprised them. It was what lay on that sea, bobbing up and down ever so slightly on the dark wavelets. In the very same instant that Nairs collected himself and hissed 'Down ... *hit the deck everybody!*' he heard that same sound he had that night in the bungalow forty-eight hours before.

A dark shadow dragged itself over their crouched bodies, the pilot obviously throttling back his twin engines as he came in to land. A couple of moments later the seaplane was skidding across the surface of the Gulf, trailing a white bubbling wake behind it, to come to a halt next to the little tender surrounded by its anchored charges. And even before Nairs could identify the seaplanes aloud for the benefit of the rest of the patrol, Nobby Clark beat him to it. 'Great balls of frigging fire,' he exclaimed, almost swallowing his words with excitement, his prominent Adam's apple racing up and down his skinny throat like an express lift. '*Nips ... Nips ... every-bleeding-where*'

Book One: Death Patrol

One

He rose from the bath like a pink happy hippo and scattered water all around him as he stepped out and reached for the whisky and the big Cuban cigar that were waiting for him. Immediately the attentive valet started patting his totally hairless body with the big white towel like some anxious mother worried that her baby might catch cold in the nude. The old man didn't even notice. But then all his life he had never noticed servants and petty details of that nature. They had been there when he had needed them. That was all that had ever concerned him.

Field Marshal Brooke looked away. Prudish Ulsterman that he was, he didn't like the sight of a naked body even when it belonged to an old man such as this.

Admiral Pound of the Royal Navy, big, bluff hands in the pockets of his reefer, as if he were still back on the quarterdeck of the battlewagon, he had once commanded, guffawed to himself. The Old Man was a real card, he told himself. Didn't give a damn what people thought of him.

Another servant appeared as if from nowhere and lit the old man's cigar. He gave it a preliminary happy puff, still apparently not noticing the second servant and reached for his whisky. A second towel was draped around his very white, hairless body, somehow leaving his loins free. He looked down and chuckled with his toothless mouth.

'Never fear, Brookie,' he lisped to the embarrassed Army's Chief-of-Staff, 'that particular pigeon won't ever fly again.' He pulled the towel closed to indicate what 'pigeon' he meant.

Pound laughed, the hearty, easy laugh of a man well pleased with himself, and said, 'I'm afraid I'm heading that particular way myself, Prime Minister. It's inevitable I suppose, at our age.'

Winston Churchill, the British Prime Minister, ignored the comment. Sex had never been a particular interest of his. His whole life had been dominated by politics. He slipped in the false teeth proferred him on a silver tray by the second valet, dismissed both of them with a casual wave of his cigar and they disappeared as silently as they had appeared.

'Now,' he said in that familiar, spine-chilling growl of his, as they closed the door behind them silently again, 'what news from our eastern empire? What are the little yellow people up to, Brookie, eh?' He looked pointedly at Brooke.

Brooke, who fervently wished the PM wouldn't receive them in his bathroom here at Chequers – he'd be lecturing them next on the 'throne' of his thunderbox if this went on – cleared his throat. 'Intelligence reports that their radio traffic in the area has increased threefold in the last forty-eight hours and our spies in China tell us that they are rushing troop trains southwards from that country almost hourly. They're building up to something, Prime Minister.'

Churchill dipped the end of his cigar in the whisky thoughtfully, twirled it round a couple of times and finally said, 'What do Ultra and Magic say?' He meant the two great Anglo-American decoding operations.

'Virtually the same thing. More details of

the big build-up in the general area of Indo-China and the Gulf of Siam.'

This time Churchill didn't ponder. Instead he turned with surprising speed for such an old man and rasped at Pound, who was caught a little off guard, 'Well, Pound, what do you make of that, eh?' His tone was almost accusing.

Pound, flushing a little red, spluttered, 'Damned difficult to say, without being on the spot, PM. But our educated guess – the Sea Lords and Naval Intelligence, that is, is–' he frowned and hesitated.

Churchill as always was quick off the mark. 'Come on, Pound,' he snapped, 'pee or get off the pot, as our American cousins say.'

Pound blurted it out and Brooke was pleased at his sudden discomfiture. It was good to see the Senior Service being taken down a peg or two by Winnie for a change. 'All-out attack, sir! The Nips' objective is obvious. Since the Yanks started starving them of rubber and other strategic goods by their export embargo, the Nips have been desperate for rubber, tin and the like. Malaya–'

'Yes, Malaya would provide them with those strategic war materials,' Churchill interrupted him calmly. 'So it's Malaya, then, eh?'

'We think so.'

Still carrying his glass and cigar, Churchill stumped barefoot, trailing drops of water as he did so, to the map pinned to the wall of the bathroom. It was typical of him, Brooke told himself. The PM had maps everywhere. He probably had one in his thunderbox.

Pensively he stared at the map while the two service chiefs waited in silence. Down on the road beyond Churchill's home, a company of Home Guard was swinging by, singing lustily for such old men, *'And this is number four, an' I've got her on the floor ... roll me over, lay me down and do it agen ... Roll me over in the clover...'*

Brooke frowned. But then he concentrated on the great man, as he turned and announced in that sonorous voice of his, which had rallied the nation in those dark days after Dunkirk the year before, 'I agree. It's Malaya. Indeed I shall tell you something which you'll keep under your hats for the time being, but which the whole world will know only too soon – President Roosevelt thinks the little yellow men are readying for an all-out attack on both America *and* the Empire in the Far East.'

Pound pouted his lips and said contemptuously, 'Wouldn't take it too seriously, sir. The Nips are all four-eyed, can't damn well shoot straight to save their lives. Why, in my youth they still went to war carrying parasols made of rice paper in case it rained. We'd soon see 'em off, if they did do anything as foolish as to attack the British Empire.'

Churchill didn't look convinced. But he didn't comment on the Admiral's words. Instead he said, 'What's the Army's position, Brookie?'

Brooke knew the PM had the facts at his fingertips already – he always had – but he took a malicious glee in attempting to discover whether his service chiefs had, too. Swiftly the field marshal reeled off the facts and the state of the various British garrisons overseas, while the PM listened attentively.

'So we can regard the Hong Kong garrison as finished the minute the little yellow men attack,' he concluded. 'Malaya itself is under strength. But I approve the sending of the British 18th Infantry Division to that country at once.'

Brooke nodded, though he didn't like the idea one bit. It was like throwing good money after bad. The 20,000 strong British division could well be destroyed within days of arriving in the Far East if the balloon went up before they got used to the climate, the conditions and settled in. But still he said nothing as the PM announced carefully, 'So, in essence, everything depends upon Singapore, here, doesn't it, gentlemen?' He placed his pudgy hand to cover the great British naval base in the far East – some even said the greatest in the world.

They nodded.

Pound opened his mouth, after Churchill didn't speak, then thought better of it and said nothing. A row had been raging between the Admiralty and the PM for months now about the naval strength needed in Singapore waters as a deterrent to the Japs. Churchill wanted the Navy's newest warship, the 35,000 ton *Prince of Wales*, plus the World War One vintage fast battlecruiser, the *Repulse*, to be stationed out there as a major force. Their Lordships were against it. The *Prince of Wales* was a fine ship, they knew that, perhaps the best modern battleship in the world. But the steel monster, launched and commissioned only months before, had to be proved.

Indeed she had been dispatched to fight

the *Bismarck* still so new that she had had one hundred civilian shipbuilder's men on board. How surprised they had been – these middle-aged civvies – to find themselves suddenly in the middle of a great naval battle. Pound smiled mildly at the thought, but his smile vanished the very next instant. In that battle, five of her ten main guns had suffered mechanical breakdowns before the ship had had time for 'working up'. And still the *Prince of Wales,* in their Lordships' expert opinion, was not fit for battle, especially against a great navy as that possessed by the Japs.

All the same, Pound told himself, as he continued to wait for the PM to speak, that didn't count much with Churchill. The *Prince of Wales,* which recently had taken him to meet President Roosevelt off Newfoundland where the two of them had formulated the Atlantic Charter, was his favourite naval ship. Indeed, while the pro-Churchill faction in the Navy (usually the lower deck, naturally) called the *Wales,* HMS Unsinkable, the opposition (upper deck), on the other hand entitled her maliciously 'Churchill's Yacht'. Naturally that name pleased the PM, who knew everything.

27

Finally Churchill broke the brooding silence of the place, speaking slowly, as if he were formulating his ideas while he spoke. 'I know everyone thinks Singapore is impregnable. It should be – the money we've spent on the place in the last decade.' He frowned. 'But I can't take chances. Not only is it a matter of prestige that we do not lose Singapore if the Japs attack Malaya, but it is of vital–'

'You're not, sir,' Pound broke in urgently, unable to contain himself any longer in his anxiety, 'you're not going to send "Force Z" to Singapore?' He meant the *Wales* and the *Repulse*. 'Two ships without destroyer escort and adequate air cover?'

Brooke looked at his colleague with surprise, but understanding. Nobody ever interrupted the PM. Pound must be at the end of his tether to do so.

Churchill nodded solemnly. 'I am ... it is a risk that must be taken, Pound.' He didn't seem surprised at Pound's outburst; it was almost as if he had expected it. 'We must hedge our bets. You understand, don't you...' The PM's voice faltered for a moment and suddenly Brooke, not an emotional man, felt sorry for him. He knew the great burdens that rested on Churchill's

28

shoulders, and he was not a young man.

Surprised at himself, he heard himself saying, 'We understand, sir. Singapore is more than just a bastion of the Empire, it is a *symbol* of it as well. If Singapore fell to the Nips...' he shook his head, 'it doesn't bear thinking about, sir.'

'Exactly, Brookie. Thank you for your understanding. It is for that reason that we must risk "Force Z". But,' he raised one pudgy finger like a pale pork sausage in warning, 'we must not let the little yellow men learn that we are sending out two of our capital ships without a destroyer escort and with just a handful of aircraft to protect them.'

Pound said, 'It takes capital ships to sink capital ships, sir. Planes alone could not do it.'

But no one was listening to him now. Instead Brooke and Churchill were staring at the map on the wall, as if they could see something there known only to them. Finally Brooke spoke what the Prime Minister was thinking. 'Let's hope that "Tom Thumb" gets them there in time.' He meant Admiral Sir Tom Phillips, commander of the British Eastern Fleet, known on account of his diminutive size

29

throughout the fleet as 'Admiral Tom Thumb'.

'Yes, now it all depends on "Tom Thumb",' Churchill agreed and, abruptly seized with an aggressive burst of energy known only to himself, he drained the rest of his whisky and dashed the glass at the bath where it shattered.

It was Friday, 29 November 1941. The decision had been made...

Two

Like silent grey ghosts, the two great ships slid through the milky-white of the dawn mist. An hour before the fog had come drifting in from the east. At first it had been nothing more than a few grey wisps, curling themselves silently, gently, softly, almost unnoticed about the two capital ships heading north. But slowly, as the day had approached and it had begun to grow hotter with the abrupt intensity of the tropics, the fog had thickened. Now it drowned all sound, save perhaps the steady throb of the ships' great engines, the mechanical heart of these bringers of death and sudden destruction.

Down below in 'A' Division Mess, the three-striper 'Big Slack Arse', still sipping his battered mug of 'gash' tea,★ said to his oppo, 'Little Slack Arse', another wizened three-striper like himself, 'What d'yer think, bird brain?'

★Gash, naval slang for 'free, extra' etc.

31

'Little Slack Arse', a twenty-one-year man, put back his set of issue false teeth and answered, 'I ain't paid to think, yer know that, matey. Leave that to the skipper and "Tom Thumb".'

By way of comment, 'Big Slack Arse' extended a long dirty middle finger.

His oppo wasn't offended. He said routinely, 'Can't, old mucker. Got a frigging great double-decker bus up there already – courtesy London Transport.'

'Frigging cockneys,' his mate said without rancour. 'Lot o' frigging nancy boys. You–' He paused suddenly. A young sailor, dressed in his anti-flash gear, complete with gas mask bag slung across his chest, was hurrying through the mess, dodging the unstowed hammocks everywhere like some medieval man-at-arms hurrying into battle. 'Hey, hold yer hosses there, matey,' 'Big Slack Arse' called, 'Hey, you H.O.* What yer frigging rushing around like a blue-arsed fly?'

The rating stopped dead. Like all H.O. men he was wary of these old stripeys who seemed to have been in the Royal Navy since Nelson's time. 'Going to me post,

*Hostilities Only, i.e. wartime service only rating.

32

Stripey,' he said plaintively.

'I know,' 'Big Slack Arse' mimicked his tone, 'didn't think yer was going to the heads for a crafty wank, like. What's it like up top?' he added as the handsome young sailor blushed deeply.

'Same as before, Stripey. Our Chiefie' – he meant chief petty officer – 'sez the skipper is still trying to get a fix on whoever's out there. And this fog ain't helping much, is it?'

The two old sea dogs didn't answer his question. Instead they waved lazy hands for him to go, with 'Little Slack Arse' aping an officer and crying, 'Oh, do carry on, rating. Just don't stand there talking.'

The relieved rating fled, while the stripey with the false teeth produced a can of evaporated milk and proceeded to open it with his jack-knife, saying, 'Half-inched this from them thieving cooks in the galley. Pass the tea bucket. Might as well make oursens comfy while Tom Thumb makes up his mind, matey.'

Obediently the other old sailor held up the tea bucket. He had seen it all before; he was bored...

Admiral Sir Tom Phillips, known throughout the Navy as 'Tom Thumb', wasn't. In

33

fact, the little Fleet Commander was nervous and on his toes, though he didn't show that to the captain of the *Prince of Wales*. That would have been 'decidedly bad form', as he would have phrased it. Instead, together with Captain John Leach, he focused his glasses on the shimmering milk-white surface of the sea, while behind him in the bridge radar shack, sweating officers and ratings tried to pick up the unknown intruder once again.

Half an hour before, just as he was finishing off his second cup of tea and wondering whether he should ask the mess steward for another piece of the excellent buttered toast, the asdic report had come in and driven all thought of further food and drink from his mind. It had been short and startling in its brutality: 'Getting a signal, sir.'

Immediately the little admiral had asked for confirmation, barking to the Marine messenger, 'And make sure it isn't a bloody shoal of fish.'

It hadn't been. Minutes later the alarms had started to sound. The Marine bugler had blown 'action stations' over the tannoy system and ratings had run back and forth along the upper deck, ringing and sounding their alert triangles for those who couldn't hear the tannoy. Immediately the great 35,000 ton ship had been the scene of controlled chaos, with sailors in anti-flash gear pelting to their stations in the huge turrets, anti-aircraft gunners swinging themselves behind their bofors and 'Chicago pianos'*, fire control parties unrolling their hoses – the hundred and one tasks that had to be completed at the double as a ship went into action.

Thereafter, in the echoing silence aboard the battleship, they had settled down to wait, each man wrapped in a cocoon of his own fears, thoughts and apprehensions, as the *Wales* ploughed steadily north-east through the mist.

Now the little Admiral said, 'If it *is* a sub, who's it belong to? The Huns do you think, John?'

Leach, tall, elegant in the traditional naval fashion, but as hard as steel, shook his head. 'Doubt it, Admiral. We know, of course, that the Jerries have a few long-range vessels – big devils. But they are used strictly for supply and cargo carrying. Underwater mother ships, you might call them.'

*Banks of massed machine-guns.

Admiral Sir Tom Phillips nodded, but he didn't cease his scrutiny of that dead, white, lifeless seascape. He knew that the whole of the Far East might well depend upon his getting these two great ships into the waters off Malaya. He couldn't afford to make the slightest mistake. 'But if it isn't the Hun, could it be the Japs? We'll discount the Eyeties. They're brave, but this is too far afield for them, you know.'

'Could be, sir. But I doubt it. I don't think the Japs would show their hand so soon. But you never know.'

'Agreed, John. Wouldn't trust the Nips with a barge pole. After all they did sink the Russian fleet back in 1905 without warning. You can't–'

He stopped short as down below on the after deck a lookout sang out suddenly, 'Sub ... *sub to port bow!*'

Leach was about to curse at the sloppy way the lookout was reporting his sighting, but he didn't get a chance to. Next to him the little admiral flung a hurried look around the great bridge, the officers' faces set and tense as they peered at their instruments, ready at a moment's notice to spring into action and respond to orders, and cried, 'Port twenty... Let's have a bloody good look-see, eh!'

Leach didn't get a chance to reply as his bridge officers cried out their orders to helmsman and engine crew, the telegraph clanging, the man at the plot yelling out his changes.

Swiftly, as if on some order from on high, the fog started to clear and the great 35,000 ton ship began to swing round ready for action. *'Guns,'* Leach came to life, hands cupped around his mouth, shouting with all his strength against the sudden breeze, 'stand by for surface action... *Local control... Stand by!'*

The gunners behind their small cannon and massed machine-guns needed no urging. The tension, nerve-racking as it had been for the last half an hour, was broken at last. Behind their weapons, the gun-layers screwed their right eyes to the rubber pads of their sights, waiting for the first indication of the enemy. And there it was. Even as the brawny gun crew cradled the big shells to their arms, ready to reload in a flash, for they knew their very lives might depend upon their speed, an evil grey shape slid into the shining calibrated glass circle of the guns' sights. 'Sub,' someone yelled, as if it were an achievement to identify the craft which they had all expected, 'A BLEEDING SUB!'

On the bridge, the two senior officers flung up their big binoculars once more in the same gesture. Hastily they fiddled with the range. And there it was. Grey, ugly, sinister – a submarine.

'Christ Almighty!' the little admiral said as he identified the limp red-white-and-blue flag hanging at its bow. 'IT'S A FROG ... A FROG SUB'

'You can't trust the Frogs, sir,' Leach gasped. 'I don't think they ever got over Nelson and the Battle of Trafalgar. However since–'*

He never finished the sentence. The French submarine, becalmed on the surface for some reason – perhaps it had been recharging its electric batteries – opened fire.

Furious white criss-crossing lines raced towards the great ship. They grew in speed by

*A beaten France had got out of the war with Germany in the summer of 1940. Since that time the rump of France, known as Vichy France had been actively anti-British, fighting against Britain in Syria and Iraq, and once actually bombing Gibraltar.

the second. Down below 'Big Slack Arse' cried, in mock piety, 'For what we're about to receive, may the Good Lord make us truly thank–'

Like an iron stick being run along some iron railing, shrapnel pattered the length of the *Prince of Wales*. At the stern, a cook throwing slops overboard stopped abruptly, the bucket falling from his hand. He looked down at his white apron, suddenly stained a dark red, as if he couldn't believe this was happening to him. Next moment he pitched wordlessly over the rail to the water far below.

Next moment, the gunners on the *Prince of Wales* opened up. The world erupted into violent noise. The port side of the great ship disappeared in belches of dark smoke as tongues of scarlet flame leapt out of cannon everywhere. That first terrible salvo was followed by the racket of a gun turret opening fire. There was the sound of what might be a huge piece of canvas being ripped apart. Again flame stabbed the smoke.

One ... two ... three ... four ... The heavy shells fell short. They struck the surface of the sea. Huge gouts of boiling water shot upwards in a white fury. The unknown sub heeled crazily. For a moment it disappeared from view.

Hurriedly, steadying himself on the heeling deck, the little admiral spun the wheel of his binoculars around, focusing them once more, speaking above the crazy racket, 'Good ... we've sunk the Frog bastard... That solves the diplomatic problem of what to do with–' The words died on his lips. The water showered down with a great slithering roar to reveal the submarine still wallowing in the trough.

Next to the Admiral, Leach cursed and cried, 'The bugger hasn't gone under yet – damn her to hell!'

Down below the gunners worked flat out. Sweating heavily, their faces under the white flash hoods looking as if they had been greased with Vaseline, they reloaded frantically, thrusting home the wads of explosive, ramming them into the tube with their rods, slamming in new shells.

Three hundred yards away the unknown skipper of the sub tried his best, knowing what was soon to come. He swung his crippled craft round. Now he was bows on to the *Prince of Wales*, thus presenting the smallest possible target. An instant later a star shell exploded directly above the battleship's bridge, bathing all below in its hard, unreal, glacial light.

'The sod's going to have a go at us,' Leach yelled in surprise and alarm.

The little admiral yelled a new course to the senior helmsman. Frantically the wrinkled CPO did as he was ordered. Already there was that familiar frightening flurry of bubbles at the stricken sub's bow, indicating that she had fired her forward torpedoes.

'Stand by,' the officer-of-the-watch yelled madly, 'here come the frigging tin fish!'

The little admiral knew this was not naval fashion, according to King's Regulations, but he could understand the frantic young officer. The situation was very nip and tuck. One false move, one slightest slip, and the pride of the Royal Navy, the *Wales*, would never reach its destination.

Now the skipper of the mysterious sub flying the French tricolour had his machine-gunners on deck, firing away at the superstructure of the great battle-ship towering above them. They hosed the ship. Tracer howled off the steel. A wire rope holding a lifeboat in place was severed. The boat sagged and toppled to the heaving water. A radio mast came down, all confused rigging and wires, blue sparks flashing and erupting angrily everywhere.

The little admiral cursed. He knew what the submarine skipper was after. He was desperately trying to disrupt the bridge and gunners, get them off their mark, giving his damned tin fish time to strike home.

But that wasn't to be. He caught a flash of exploding bubbles far below on the surface of the sea, and the torpedoes were hurtling past the *Prince of Wales* purposelessly. Next instant a 4.5-inch shell slammed right into the sub's conning tower, a ball of angry flame. What looked like a great mushroom made of white smoke rose staidly from the conning tower and the deadly little craft came to an abrupt stop, water pouring into the great gash ripped in her steel side.

The little admiral hesitated only a fraction of a second. He knew that the sub was finished. She presented no danger any more. Her skipper had shot his bolt. All that was left to him now was to surrender himself – if he were still alive – and the survivors. Now it was up to him to play the gallant rescuer. But could he afford to do so? There was more at stake than just the decency and respect which had always existed between sailors whatever their nationality and whether or not they were enemies. After all, the sea itself was their common enemy, wasn't it?

Captain Leach looked at him. 'Shall we stand by to pick up survivors, Admiral?' he asked. 'She'll be going under soon.' He indicated the crippled sub, her long evil-looking bow already awash, with a few pathetic souls clutching the shattered conning tower, here and there one of them waving a singlet in token of surrender. 'Shouldn't take us more than half an hour and I could send up the Walrus,' – he meant the ship's ancient spotter flying boat – 'to check and secure the area while we do so.'

The little admiral made his decision. 'No,' he said, his face revealing nothing.

'What?' Leach asked aghast.

'No,' the admiral repeated. 'No survivors.' He turned on his heel and then almost as if it was an after-thought, he announced through gritted teeth, *Ram and sink the bugger!* With that he strode away leaving the *Prince of Wales* crew to stare at his skinny shoulders in total, absolute disbelief...

Three

In silence the two senior officers sipped their pink gins (although it was only ten o'clock in the morning) and tried to ignore the cloying stink of ether and urine that filled the stifling air of the sick bay.

The surgeon-commander looked at the two blanket-shrouded figures on the wet-red floor of the sick bay and then at the two senior officers. He was slight and bespectacled, but the little admiral, who had served with the doctor, knew just how tough he was. He had already won the DSC back in 1940 for amputating a rating's leg half underwater in a destroyer that was about to go to the bottom. 'Are you ready, gentlemen?'

The admiral muttered, 'Yes' and took a hasty drink at his pink gin. He had seen enough dead bodies in his time, but he still didn't like the sight of 'stiffs'. Outside some deckhand was singing wearily, *'I've got spurs that jingle-jangle, as I ride merrily along...'* The admiral dearly would have loved to have shouted at him to shut up, but he knew that that would be seen as nerves. In an hour it would be all around the ship, 'Tom Thumb's gorn and lost his nerve.' He couldn't have that.

The surgeon-commander turned to the sick bay attendant in his blood-stained apron and commanded, 'All right, Joe ... the first one.'

'Ay, ay, sir,' he answered. Deftly the rating whipped away the blanket covering the first dead man.

Captain Leach gasped. The body had no head. Where the head had been there was a jagged dull red gap, which had been plugged with a blood-red hand towel.

The surgeon-commander didn't seem to notice his shock or the fact the corpse was minus a head. Instead he lectured them as if they were a couple of especially thick medical students. 'You will note that the body is not very muscular and very white. In addition it has no tattooes or the usual things that regular sailors – and sub-mariners are usually regulars – pick up during the course of their career.'

'Among other things, such as – er – anti-social diseases, what, doctor?' The little admiral attempted a little forced humour to relieve the tension.

The surgeon-commander didn't seem to hear. Instead he continued with, 'From this I conclude the man was an officer, perhaps even the skipper of the sub. And you'll notice the nails. Very well kept and manicured. Hence an officer – and a Frenchman, too, of course.'

'A Frenchman – how do you know that, doctor? I know we spotted the French tricolour. But how do you know that about this poor chap in particular?' The little admiral frowned and waited.

'Easy,' came the confident reply. The doctor indicated the white surgical pail in the corner of the room, with what looked like a bloody football lying carelessly inside it. 'His head. I had a quick peep at his teeth. He had a gold tooth and other dental work – typically French.'

Leach didn't look. Instead he took a gulp of his pink gin and asked swiftly, 'And the other corpse?'

The bespectacled doctor's face brightened. 'Now that's more like it, gentlemen,' he said heartily, as if he had discovered a sudden cure for cancer overnight. The little admiral cursed all hearty naval sawbones and waited.

Again the doctor nodded to the sombre-faced sick-bay attendant. He covered the first corpse once again and then with a sweeping movement like a waiter putting on a new tablecloth for the benefit of an honoured client who tipped well, he pulled the blanket from the second corpse.

The doctor looked at it and the two senior officers for their reaction, and then said in a kind of mock cockney, 'Now there's a turn-up for the books, gentleman. Not 'arf, eh?'

It was. The second corpse – short, squat and yellow-skinned, with no identification or indication of how he had died – was certainly that of an Oriental.

The doctor saw their puzzled looks and answered their question even before they could pose it. 'So what is he? Is he a Chink or a Jap – and more importantly, what was he doing on a French sub?' He beamed at them, let his words sink in and then spoke. 'As you gentlemen well know, we use Chinamen on His Majesty's vessels quite a lot out here in the East. There must be thousands of chinks serving as stewards, dhobi wallahs and the like on the China Station alone. So do the French do the same?' He shrugged and answered his own question, 'I don't know. All I do know is that this chap isn't a Chink.'

'How do you know, Commander?' the admiral asked severely, a little sick of the doctor playing damned Sherlock Holmes. 'I can never bloody well tell the difference.'

The medic was patient. 'Look at the feet, sir, if you would.' He reached across and held up the corpse's left foot, as if he might an infected sailor's penis during a short arm inspection.*

'What about his bloody feet?' Leach exclaimed a little angrily. He was sick in both senses of the word at the whole business.

Obviously the surgeon-commander loved his newly acquired role as the Sherlock Holmes of HMS *Prince of Wales*, for, in no way offended, he said airily, 'Just look at his toes, gentlemen.'

They did and after a moment the little admiral grunted. 'So he's got ten like the rest of us.'

'Yes, sir, but look how the big toe and the one next to it are parted.'

'So?'

'Well, that comes from wearing a special shoe – the '*zarie*', the Japs called it, I recall,

---

*Inspection for VD.

when I was last at Yokohama. It's a split shoe into which you shove the big toe and the one next to it separately, with the thong that secures the shoe coming down in between the two of them.'

The little admiral said quickly. 'So this chap,' he indicated the corpse, 'isn't a Chink. He's a Nip.'

'Yes sir – and a special one, as far as we are concerned.'

'And what's that supposed to mean,' Leach demanded, at the end of his patience now.

'The shoe indicates he's a Jap and the imprint of the nails beneath the sole,' he held up the man's left foot for them to see the marks left by the boot there, 'plus the harder skin at the ball of the foot and the heel tell us something else.'

'Oh, do get on with it, Commander,' the admiral pleaded, 'I haven't got all the bloody time in the world, you know.'

'Sorry, sir. Yessir. Well, sir,' the doctor said in somewhat of a rush now, for he didn't need to be Conan Doyle's celebrated detective to recognize that the Admiral was swiftly running out of patience. 'All these factors suggest one thing,' he hesitated only a fraction of a second before plunging on to his final conclusion. 'This chap was probably a Jap officer. On the right hip you can see the permanent bruise where his sword has constantly banged against his side and in the Jap Army only officers wear a sword.'

'*Christ All-bloody-Mighty!*' Leach exploded, as the sick-bay attendant drew the bloodstained blanket across the sightless slant eyes once more. 'What the devil's going on...?'

Now as the *Prince of Wales* pounded on, getting ever closer to her date with destiny, the two senior officers considered. Anyone seeing them crouched there over the maps spread out on the battered wardroom table could have told, without a word being said on their part, that they were worried men. More than that – they were very puzzled men, for as the little admiral exclaimed yet again, 'What the devil are the Nips – an army officer to boot – doing on board a Frog sub? As you know, John, the Nips have the Frogs in their pocket now, especially the French Navy. That Frog admiral of theirs–'

'Admiral Darlan, sir.'★

'Yes, that chap hates our guts with a passion.

★Footnote on next page

50

He's helped the Huns against us in the past. So I'd not be surprised if he would help the Nips against us now.' The admiral shrugged his little shoulders helplessly. 'But in what form is the French Navy prepared to help the Nips? That's beyond me at this stage of the game.'

Leach sighed heavily. 'Me, too, sir. But I don't think we can do much about it, don't you think, until we know more. I 'spect it'll all come out in the wash in the end.'

The admiral pulled himself together. 'You're right, of course, John, as usual.'

It was just about then that Jenkins knocked and without really waiting for permission entered the admiral's cabin, bearing a silver platter and a bottle of Haig. 'Thought you might like some food, gentlemen,' he announced. 'Pork pies. The galley wallahs have just made them.'

The admiral, who had a sensitive stomach, eyed them warily. 'Pork in this climate?' he queried.

*Darlan, a senior minister in the renegade French Vichy Government, who hated the British but who in 1942 finally went over to the Allies in North Africa when the War was turning in their favour. He was assassinated shortly afterwards.

'All taken care of, sir,' Jenkins answered airily, flipping back the metal catch of the bottle of Haig. 'Don't be vague, ask for Haig,' he quoted the current slogan used by the Scottish whisky firm. 'Whisky'll settle any stomach, pork or no pork.'

'What about the liver?' Leach said, eyeing Jenkins, a tall bluff man with faded blue eyes and a big bulbous drinker's red nose. The commander had spent a lifetime at sea in both the Royal and Merchant Navies as a specialist signals officer. He wasn't awed by anyone. Even the Lords of the Admiralty had to watch their p's and q's with Jenkins.

The commander ignored the comment. Without asking he poured the two senior officers a stiff peg of whisky, helped himself to a hot pork pie, grunted with pleasure at the taste and then, with his mouth full, he said, 'Heard the buzz about the Frog and Nip. Bad.' He swallowed and took another bite. 'Yes, damned bad.'

'Why?' the admiral finally asked, amazed apparently how the other man could polish off such a huge pork pie in a couple of bites.

'Because the Frogs know all about us – and because the airwaves have suddenly gone silent, Admiral.' He belched pleasurably.

The admiral ignored the first remark. 'What did you say, Jenkins? Airwaves gone silent?'

'Yes. Not only the Japs' radio, but that of the Frogs too. Nothing at all coming out of French Indo-China at this moment – there's nothing either since zero six hundred hours this morning.' He reached out for another pork pie, but changed his mind when he saw the look in the little admiral's eye. At such moments, he knew from past experience, old 'Tom Thumb' wasn't to be trifled with. Instead he answered the other officer's unspoken question. 'Yessir,' he said, 'I agree with you. Military traffic only goes off the air when the balloon's about to go up...' he paused, face suddenly serious, as if he were considering the full implications about what he was about to say before he said, 'and it looks, too, as if the Nips and Frogs are working hand-in-glove.'

'Yes, Jenkins, you're right,' Leach agreed, 'but in hand in glove to do what, eh?'

Jenkins had his answer ready. 'To scupper us, sir ... that's my opinion. The Frogs are about to get their own back for Mers-el-Kebir and they don't give a tuppenny toss about the way they do it, even if it means working with the Japs!' Now the big officer thought he was entitled to his pork pie. He reached out, grabbed one and took an enormous bite out of it, the crumbs of pastry suddenly exploding all about his lips.

The little admiral no longer noticed. He was concentrating on the task in hand. Jenkins, old boozer and skirt-chaser that he was, was right, of course. There was stormy bloody work ahead and he'd better be prepared for it. If Britain lost the *Wales* and *Repulse* out here, there'd be nothing to replace them. The cupboard was bare. He shuddered a little at the thought as a cold finger of fear traced its way down the centre of his spine. With an effort he dismissed his apprehensions and fears and started to issue his new orders. Outside the cleaner reappeared. Now he had forgotten those 'spurs which jingle-jingle-jangled' as he 'rode merrily along'. Instead, in a mock *basso profundo,* he was mouthing that dire Victorian dirge of *'Down among the dead men'*.

Admiral 'Tom Thumb' shivered again...

Four

The great grey rat faced him in the diffuse light that filtered in beneath the longhouse on stilts. Its whiskers twitched. Its wickedly sharp teeth displayed hideously as it stared at the intruder in beady-eyed menace. 'Cor ferk a duck,' Nobby Clark breathed behind him, as he crouched there in the stinking green mud, 'it's as big as a ferking nag. What a long tail!'

'Shut up,' Nairs commanded, keeping his voice low. A group of the yellow men and their European companions were less than fifty yards away as they balanced on a float, working on one of the seaplane's engines. 'Keep it down to a dull roar, will you.'

He moved forward a few more paces, crawling through the clinging mud, full of human droppings from the hut above, fighting back the vomit and his fear of the grey scampering rats which were everywhere, living off the waste and food rubbish. Behind him his old batman, his heart thudding violently – for he hated what he

55

called 'longtails' with great passion – followed hesitantly, trying to keep his Lee Enfield out of the mud.

Fifteen minutes before they had left the Malay Scouts spread out in a rough-and-ready perimeter line under the cover of the edge of the mangrove swamp facing the sea. He had ordered the corporal in charge, one of his own plantation boys, to fall back with the men and relay the news – via Susi – to Colonel Hathaway, if he and Nobby didn't return before the sun reached its zenith. They would recce this strange unexpected seaplane base a little further.

Now they advanced again, apeing the young boys they had seen on the Western Front in the trenches, out beyond the wire, on a raid 'to bag a Jerry'. As Nairs had explained it to Nobby after they had set off, 'Old business, Nobby. Through the back door and not the front – you know why, old chap?'

Nobby did. Most 'snatch patrols' in the last war had failed because inexperienced officers had tried to grab a prisoner from a front-line trench. 'Mr Nairs', as Nobby had called the young Fusilier officer then, had had a different approach: 'Round the front line and into the reserve trench,' he had always maintained. 'The blokes in the front line trench are looking towards us. They're on their toes. They're *expecting* trouble. Not so in the reserve line. They think they're being taken care of by the chaps in front of them.' Now they were swinging beneath the 'longhouse' which was closest to where the strangers were working on their seaplanes in the hope they'd find someone to the rear – a cook, man off guard and the like – who could be easily seized and spirited away before anyone had noticed.

In the lead, Nairs put down his foot gingerly. Again myriads of rats broke cover and scampered away. He bent his head instinctively, fighting off the wave of revulsion, and prayed that one wouldn't drop on his bare head from the low matting roof above him. He wouldn't be able to keep quiet if it did, he knew that.

But Nairs was in luck. The rats stayed on the ground, slithering through the mud and faeces, and slowly it was beginning to grow brighter. They were coming to the far end of the longhouse, perched on its rickety, salt-and-shell encrusted stilts. Behind him Nobby saw that, too. He clutched his revolver more tightly in a hand that was hot and damp with sweat. Nairs, for his part, was going to employ another weapon when it came to snatching the, as yet unknown, prisoner.

It was a thuggee cord – a small length of tough yellow cloth, that might have been mistaken for a crude handkerchief, but one which would have put the fear of death into any older Indian seeing it. For the traditional Indian thugs and highwaymen used it, weighted by lead at one end, to wrap round their victim's throat, break his neck and steal the dead man's purse. It was cruel and vicious, Nairs knew, as he now tested the weighted strip of tough cloth, but it was swift and silent. With just the right amount of pressure applied, he recognized he could have his victim rendered half-conscious and tame within thirty seconds at the most.

They came out into the open and crouched in the shelter of the hut, blinking a little in the sudden glare of the sun. The compound seemed empty. There were a few skinny chickens scratching around the dirt hopefully. A skinny-ribbed dog lolled, eyes closed and panting in the shade of a bamboo; and from one of the women's huts on the far side there came the soft muted sounds of a woman hushing her petulant baby to sleep. But where was the snatch victim they were looking for?

There was evidence enough of the strangers' presence: piles of great oil drums, a military-looking rubber dinghy pulled up the beach, long wooden boxes which Nairs guessed contained drums of ammunition for the seaplane's machine-guns. But not a human in sight. He flashed a look at Nobby's wizened face.

There was no sign of fear on his old batman's features, only an urgent look which read: 'Let's nobble somebody – *anybody* – and do a bunk toot-sweet!'

He nodded his understanding. It was his thinking exactly. Every further minute they hung around this remote place with the strangers only yards away, the more chance they ran of being discovered. A little uncertainly he looked around the circle of crude thatched huts, which obviously were a native *kampong* taken over recently by the strangers. He wondered if he dare enter one of them on the off-chance he'd find one of them he could nobble. Suddenly he tensed. A small yellow man, clad only in boots and breeches, with his braces dangling down around his thighs and with a bunch of grass in his right hand was emerging sleepily from one of the crude structures. He yawned and it was obvious he had just been wakened from a deep sleep by the call of nature.

'His nibs himself,' Nobby hissed, nudging Nairs in the ribs in his excitement.

'Yes, that's our man,' Nairs agreed and tightened his hold on the yellow cloth. 'Come on.'

Nobby needed no urging.

Hastily, bent double, the two of them slipped out of the shadows cast by the long hut and crept towards where the sleepy man had disappeared into the mangroves. The skinny dog opened one rheumy eye and stared at them momentarily. Nairs tensed. But the dog didn't bark. Instead it yawned lazily and closed its eye again. 'Lucky sod,' Nobby said to himself and then forgot the animal as he covered Nairs' back with his First World War vintage rifle.

They heard the man before they saw him. He was grunting and groaning behind a wild vine, out of sight, save for his boots. 'Hope he's got the runs,' Nobby whispered, as the two of them tensed there.

'Shut up!' Nairs answered and prepared to move. 'On three,' he hissed and under his breath he started to count off the seconds. *'One ... two ... three.'* Abruptly he broke cover.

Suddenly all was decisive, rapid movement. The little Oriental squatting on his haunches, bundle of grass for wiping still clutched in his right hand, stared up at them in wide-eyed alarm and surprise. He opened his mouth to shout. Nairs didn't give him a chance to do so. His length of yellow cloth flashed out. It caught the squatting man neatly round the neck and his cry was stifled in his throat. Next instant Nairs pulled hard. For a moment the man's face was contorted horribly. His eyes bulged. Frantically he grabbed at the cloth and tried to pull it away. To no avail! Nairs grunted and tugged harder, while Nobby watched in barely concealed horror. He'd forgotten just how tough the boss could be. The Oriental's eyelids fluttered. He made little gasping sounds. The urine poured from his naked lower body. Suddenly he went limp.

For what seemed an age, Nairs towered above him, his face flushed and contorted, his breath coming in short, sharp, hectic gasps. He seemed transfixed – in another world. They were like two lovers, clasped together in some final embrace for ever.

'Sir,' Nobby hissed urgently.

'Yes ... yes...' Nairs shook his head like a man coming back from a bad dream.

Instinctively he loosened the pressure on the other man's throat. His chest heaved. 'Good, sir,' Nobby commented. 'You ain't croaked him for good.'

Nairs nodded. He couldn't speak at that moment. Instead he released the weighted cloth, pulling hard to free it from where it had dug deeply into the unconscious man's skinny throat, his chest still heaving madly. It was as if he had just run a great race. 'Come on,' he commanded thickly.

Swiftly the two of them started to skirt the outskirts of the little hamlet, moving away from the shoreline, heading into the mangroves and the jungle. Behind them the engines of one of the seaplanes burst into noisy life and made them start. The man on Nairs' shoulder groaned faintly. But it was only the strangers seemingly testing the motors of the seaplane they were working on a hundred yards or so away.

Now they were into the jungle proper. As soon as they were away from the coolness of the sea breeze, they were struck an almost physical blow by the stifling heat of the vegetation.

Nobby gasped and told himself he'd never get used to the heat if he lived in Malaya another hundred bloody years, but somehow guessed – truthfully – he'd never survive that long. Still, he pushed on bravely, stopping momentarily every few moments, finger curled round the trigger of the rifle, to stare behind them. But they were not being followed. They were getting away with it. The 'snatch-and-scarper' job, as they had once called such things in the trenches back in 1918, seemed to be working out successfully.

But Nobby Clark was premature. They had just cleared a large area of typical mangrove swamp when they were startled by the sudden angry snap-and-crack of a firefight, through which they could hear the slow stutter of a Bren gun firing short bursts. It was the only automatic weapon the little group of Malay Scouts they had left behind to cover them possessed. Their rearguard was in trouble. More than they could cope with, it appeared. For now they could hear the soft, obscene plop and burst of light mortar shells exploding to their right. The strangers were using mortars.

'*Bollocks!*' Nairs exploded in sudden fury. 'Now that.'

'You heard right, sir ... what now?' Nobby added urgently.

Nairs made a quick decision. 'We can't get

away with this bastard, that's for sure.' He indicated the limp man slung over his shoulder. 'We wouldn't make it now.' He dropped their prisoner heavily to the ground. 'Go through his pockets, badges of rank, anything that might be useful to – you know – our intelligence people and the like.'

'Sir.' Nobby didn't need any further explanation. He knew the drill well enough. As Nairs flung a hasty glance at his map, trying to work out a route back from the sea, he went to work with a will, rifling through the now groaning man's breeches as if he were a professional pickpocket, muttering, 'Oh shut yer frigging cakehole, mate, and let me get on with it.'

Jungle, Nairs told himself, mind racing electrically, knowing as he did he had only a matter of minutes to make his decision before the strangers twigged them. 'Then back to the coast,' he muttered aloud now. 'Move quicker on the coast and–'

'Sir,' Nobby interrupted him excitedly as the man stirred yet again, till Nobby punched him and he was silent once more. 'I've found something ... a kind of silhouette with a few words of writing below ... in English–'

The slug slammed into the tree trunk next

to him, drowning the rest of his words and showering him with wood splinters. 'Cheeky bastards!' he exclaimed. 'Ain't they got no shame–'

'Come on,' Nairs rasped urgently, 'let's leg it. We'll talk later.' In the same instant that a vicious burst of machine-gun fire sliced the area where they had just been, they were up and running as if their very life depended upon it – which it did...

Five

Colonel Moto waited impatiently. He had not expected to be faced with a situation like this immediately after his arrival by seaplane from Hanoi. He had other and more important tasks in front of him in the next few days. But he was a painstaking and methodical officer. The matter had to be dealt with, although it wasted his valuable time. Subordinates had to be shown that the slightest failing on their part would be punished immediately and without mercy. At times such as this there was no place for luxuries such as mercy in the Imperial Japanese Army. The Emperor expected the utmost from his humble soldiers. Even as he thought of the Divine Being, he sucked in his breath as a sign of respect and turned automatically in what he thought would be the direction of His Majesty's palace in faraway Tokyo.

Outside men of the Kempei-tai* were

*Feared Japanese secret military policemen.

66

forcing the culprits and their associates into a three-sided formation. To his immediate front were the Japanese. To the right were the French seaplane pilots and crew, and to the left were the natives, third-class animals, Moto couldn't help thinking, though their young women were attractive enough in a barbaric uncultured way. But whatever their nationality and rank, Moto was happy to see that they were *all* afraid. That pleased him. Beneath his gleaming, polished head, his dark eyes sparkled wickedly. Automatically he brushed back his dyed black eyebrows that shot to the rear like those of some foreign devil.

The sergeant-major outside was satisfied finally. He tucked his small sword to his side and with his upper body rigid he marched to the hut, faced and bowed down, crying out so loud that the birds rose from the trees in hoarse protest. 'Parade ... all present and correct ... *sir.*'

Colonel Moto stretched himself to his full height, all five foot three inches, proudly. This was the moment he always savoured ever since he had graduated from the Imperial Cadet School in Tokyo so many years before. He placed his peaked cap firmly on his shaven gleaming skull and, grasping his samurai sword firmly by its ivory handle, marched out into the glare of the sun, snapped to attention, acknowledged the salute of the sergeant-major and stared around at the parade. He took his time, although he knew that time was running out fast. But this pedantic slowness was a sure way of undermining the confidence and steadfastness of prisoners or suspects. It had to be done – *and done properly.*

Slowly his pig-like eyes, set in a face that was expressionless and devoid of mercy, swept the ranks of the Japanese present until they lit upon the peasant-clod who had allowed himself to be taken prisoner by the intruders. The man knew he was being looked at and Colonel Moto could see him begin to quiver. That pleased him, too. He was afraid. Before he, Moto, was finished with him, he would have reason to be *very* afraid. Involuntarily he touched the hilt of his sword.

He turned his attention to the handful of French. They were much taller than the Japanese or the native animals, and were proud of themselves, he could see that. They had been allowed to retain their pistols and that made them feel even more certain of themselves, that was obvious. Moto smiled to himself. They wouldn't have felt so certain and proud if they had realised that at this very moment he had a skilled machine-gunner with his machine-gun trained on them from behind a couple of trees some hundred metres away. The gunner, at his command, could blast them away into nothingness in an instant; they deserved nothing better. God, how he hated these proud white men with their round eyes!

He beckoned to the man who had allowed himself to be captured. The man hesitated. The sergeant-major barked something in that harsh, threatening Japanese tone. The man stepped forward, marched stiffly towards Colonel Moto, both arms clasped tightly to his sides, bowed low and like some animal soon to be led off to slaughter waited for the little officer's verdict.

Not for long, however.

Moto, his evil face suffused with barely suppressed rage, stepped so close to the culprit that the man flinched and seemed about to tumble back, though he caught himself in the last moment. Moto took a firm grip on his ceremonial sword, its ivory handle beautifully worked in silver and semi-precious stones. The man's eyes bulged out of his head. Obviously he thought he was going to be beheaded on the spot.

'You let the round eye see the picture,' Moto burst out, his spittle spattering the face of the man. The latter cringed. His bottom lip trembled with fear. He tried to say something but failed.

Moto hit him across the face with his free hand. 'Speak, you son of a turd,' he cried. 'NOW!'

'Yes,' the man quavered faintly, ready to dodge a blow at any moment.

'*What?*'

'*Hai,*' the man repeated desperately.

Colonel Moto struck his side, as if he couldn't believe the evidence of his own ears. Opposite the French gaped in astonishment and bewilderment at the scene taking place before their own eyes, unable to comprehend what it was about.

'What in the name of the Gods do you think you were doing carrying the identification chart of those ships on your person?' Moto bellowed, beside himself with rage now, his hand flashing instinctively to his sword hilt, as if he would draw it at any moment and wipe off the culprit's head with one massive blow.

'I don't know,' the man said, the tears streaming down his ashen face. 'I wanted to show my comrades ... afterwards, to prove that I'd ... I wanted my village to be proud of me...' The broken sentences tumbled meaninglessly from his lips, his wet eyes full of pleading. Opposite, the senior French officer began, *'Monsieur le–'*

The enraged Moto shot him a murderous look. The Frenchman's words died on his lips. By now he had come to know – and fear – the unreasoning rages of the Japanese. Once again he cursed the day he had decided to stay loyal to Vichy because he had been complacent, enjoyed a beautiful mistress in Saigon and thought in this manner he would survive the War and live to enjoy his pension on the Côte d'Azur. He should have fled and joined de Gaulle★ and the perfidious English while he had still had the chance. Now he was too deep in with these pigs and their treacherous plot. He hawked, muttered *'sales cons!'* but when Moto looked at him again, the French officer lowered his gaze, knowing as he did

★General de Gaulle in London who was regarded as a traitor to France by the French Vichy puppet government.

so he had thrown in his lot – like most of them in Indo-China had done to save their own necks – and there was nothing to be done about it. Moto and the rest of those swaggering apes who served beneath the flag of the Rising Sun were the new masters of the East.

For a moment or two Moto continued to tremble with the sheer violence of his rage, indecisive, wondering what he should do next. He had demonstrated his power over all of them – the coolies, the round-eyes and the peasant idiots who didn't deserve to wear the honorable uniform of his Divine Majesty. Automatically he sucked in his breath as a mark of respect. Should he do it and behead the fool trembling before him, or what?

But in that same moment the decision was made for him. Out of the jungle they trooped, all of them dressed in rough Chinese clothes, yet obviously soldiers – there was no mistaking that – and surprisingly tall for Japanese. For Japanese they were, each man a member of the Imperial Guard especially trained for the bold task to come. Now those who filed behind their tall aristocratic commander carried their red bundles disdainfully like some slightly ill mother carrying an 'accident' that had just happened to one of her naughty children, who had been unable to contain himself in time.

The officer issued an order. The men stamped to a stop, each man's eyes fixed on some distant object like a good soldier's gaze should be. Moto nodded his approval and then while all around the others stared wondering what was going on, he ordered the men to lower and open their bundles.

They did so woodenly and in unison as if back in the Imperial Guard training depot they had even learned a special drill for this macabre task. In a minute they were finished. They rose as one and waited, while the others stared in horror at the objects they had been carrying in their bundles, which were now revealed for them to see.

Moto took it all in his stride. He walked the length of the bundles, staring at each grisly object in turn, his overlarge sword clanking at his hip, while the French stared and stared, their faces suddenly ashen, a mutter of stifled curses and protests running through their ranks. *'Nom de Dieu,'* their officer hissed, sickened, eyes full of disbelief. *'C'est ... c'est impossible–'*

But he was wrong. It wasn't *'impossible'*.

They were heads all right, neatly severed at the neck, as if done by some trained butcher who had calculated their weight down to the nearest milligram so that the load the men would have to carry back to the coast to report would not be excessive.

Finally Moto came to the end of the line. 'No round eyes,' he asked the young officer whose mind was already on the assault he would be seen to lead up the beach at Khota Bahru, the first English base they would capture at the start of the triumphant march on Singapore. He would die in the attempt – they all would. But the honour they would bring to their families and their native villages would make up for their early deaths. They would go down in the history books. Generations of Japanese school-children would remember as part of Japan's Imperial Destiny. They of the Imperial Guard would never be forgotten.

But Colonel Moto had other things than Japanese Imperial Destiny on his mind at that moment. It was the two white men who had seen the diagram the stupid pig cowering before him had been carrying contrary to all regulations. How the idiot had gotten away with it after all the initial recce party had been searched in Hanoi before they had set out for this remote coast, he didn't know. But he had. Now the fat was in the fire. For the patrol had indeed killed all the coolies the round eyes had brought with them. But the round eyes themselves had escaped. What was he going to do?

Already he could see himself going through the traditional ceremony of *hari-kari*, plucking a lone hair from his shaven skull, signing his will with his own blood, pulling out the little curved dagger with which he would disembowel himself and tearing it upwards savagely to enlarge the hole to make sure the blood flowed faster...

NO! a harsh little voice commanded at the back of his bullet head, *not yet!* It was not that he was afraid of dying. He, Colonel Moto, head of the 'Black Bands', the dreaded secret police, was prepared to die for the beloved Emperor at the drop of a hat. But first he wanted to see the establishment of Japan's Far Eastern Empire, the greatest since ancient times –then, and only then, he would die a happy man.

Now it was his duty to stop those two lone white men returning to the place from which they had come with their priceless information which might well destroy everything if it got into the wrong hands.

He turned once more to the young officer, who had somewhat the look of a fop about him. Moto frowned at the sight. The man well might be one of those decadent powdered creatures who preferred boys to girls. He shrugged his suspicions away. He'd soon find out where they were now going. 'Lieutenant,' he rasped, 'you will follow my command from now onwards.'

'But the reconnaissance, sir,' Imperial Guard Lieutenant Hakawaya commenced, then he saw the look on the other officer's face and the protest died in his throat.

'We know now where the enemy patrol came from,' Moto said. 'It is reasonable to expect that the round eyes will attempt to return there with their information Most of these British colonialist exploiters have radio sets. They will probably use the set there to relay their information to their higher headquarters. We must ensure they don't. Is that understood?'

'Hai!'

'Good. Then give your men fifteen minutes rest. They can eat and drink and wash–'

'The Imperial Guard needs no rest,'

Hakawaya commenced.

Moto cut him short with, 'Don't be a fool, man! Do as I say. At the double now.' He turned and looked at his sergeant-major. The man nodded. He was an old soldier. He knew what was to be done. He clicked to attention and bellowed a command.

The Japanese soldiers and airmen on parade knew what to do. They turned, saluted and marched away, followed more hesitantly by the French and the natives. But the sergeant-major knew Colonel Moto of old; they had served together long enough, right through from Manchuria into China and the 'Rape of Nanking'. Even as he crossed over to the fearful natives to pull the girl which Moto had indicated out of their ranks, he savoured those days mentally once more.

Watching the squat Japanese kicking aside the severed heads like so many abandoned footballs as he strode towards the already sobbing thirteen-year old Malay girl, Colonel Mercier, the senior officer, graduate of St Cyr, holder of the *Croix de Guerre* and *Médaille Militaire*, swallowed hard and said aloud to no one in particular, 'What have we done... Oh, my God on High, we have released the barbarians on the world...' Opposite him the old NCO was ripping open the screaming girl's top to reveal her fine young pink-tipped breasts for Colonel Moto's approval...

Six

Nairs lowered his hand slowly. In the twilight, he kept his gaze focused on the kampong. They had seen it first by the thin blue smoke rising above the canopy of jungle. But he and Nobby had hesitated about moving straight to it to ask for water and food, and shelter for the night. By now they knew there were Japs in the jungle and, to a certain extent, what their purpose was. They didn't want to bump into their pursuers for they knew what their fate would be if they did – *sudden, violent death!*

So they had skirted around the place cautiously. They had broken their way through about two miles of stinking, rotting mangroves and stunted bamboos, the big flat leaves of pulpy vegetation slapping up and down against their faces like soft blows from pudgy damp fists. Very unpleasant. But at least they knew it wasn't an approach to the kampong that the Japs would use.

Now they crouched in the undergrowth, trying to ignore the mosquitoes which were beginning to buzz everywhere, for darkness was descending with that startling suddenness of the tropics. Nobby leaned over and spoke softly into his officer's ear just as he had once done in the trenches, and even before he spoke Nairs realized they were reverting to the tough young soldiers they had once been twenty-odd years before. Nothing was being taken for granted now. In a couple of days they had shrugged off nearly a quarter of a century of civilization. Now it was kill or be killed. 'I've had a good old butcher's, sir,' he whispered. 'But apart from that smoke, I haven't dekkoed nuthin'.'

Nairs nodded his agreement. Yes, he told himself, apart from the smoke, nothing else seemed to be moving in the cluster of primitive huts located in the centre of the small marshy clearing. There were none of the usual women bringing in the water for the night; the naked kids forcing their skinny chickens into the safety of their atap huts; not even the old men smoking their cheroots in the open and drinking tin mugs of crude coffee if they were lucky enough to get that particular treat. 'What do you think, Nobby?' he broke the silence after a while, knowing as he posed the question that they couldn't afford to run any risks now that they knew what they did.

'Well, sir,' his ex-batman answered, pleased that the major had *asked* him and not *told* him what they were going to do. 'It looks a bit doubtful to Mrs Clark's handsome son, but I think we could use some grub and rest–'

'Yes, and some advice on how to get to Khota Baru,' he meant the nearest British base on the Gulf of Siam.

'Yessir. So I say we risk it. The frigging Nips can't be everywhere.' He looked up at the officer through the growing gloom, a winning look on his wizened, skinny face.

'Agreed. But I can't guarantee any ale,' Nairs said with a fleeting grin.

'Don't even mention wallop, sir,' Nobby said heartily. 'Yer'll have me innards doing backflips if yer do.'

'All right,' Nairs said, rising to his feet, his mind made up, 'follow me. But keep yer eyes peeled.'

'Like the proverbial tinned tomatoes, sir,' Nobby said and, unslinging his rifle, clicked off the safety catch.

Together, with Nairs in the lead, the canvas top of his revolver holster open just in case, they advanced on the silent village in the middle of nowhere.

Now the bats were flying low, zipping by and just missing their heads. Somewhere monkeys were screeching frantically, as if they were in mortal agony. But the two white men didn't seem to notice; their attention was directed on the kampong almost exclusively. Slowly but surely they forced their way through the thick matted foliage to the rear of the place, trying to ignore the still thick, clammy, greenhouse heat. And then they were through. Before them lay the circle of huts. No sign of life as yet, although the thin trickle of grey smoke rose lazily from the holes in the thatched roofs.

They paused, a little uncertain. 'Funny turn up for the books, sir,' Nobby commented in a whisper.

'You're right–' Nairs commenced and stopped short. Lying to the right of the nearest hut a body was stretched out in the dust, hardly visible now that it was getting dark so quickly. 'What in God's name is that?'

'A bint, sir–' Nobby choked for a moment as he made out the girl, lying stretched out naked. She had been split cleanly from breast to abdomen in what must have been a single blow from a very sharp sword. But it wasn't that which made the two observers suddenly feel violently sick. It was the object inside her, over which the fat, greedy flies buzzed in ghoulish profusion. 'Oh my God,' Nobby said thickly, holding his hand abruptly to his mouth, as if he were going to retch, 'the poor thing was pregnant!'

Slowly, like two provincials mesmerized by a third-class hypnotist in some rundown Hippodrome, they advanced on the slaughtered girl, Nobby Clark attempting to shoo away the greedy, buzzing flies with a feeble wave of his free hand. They stared down at her numbly. She could hardly have been older than fourteen to judge by her small girlish breasts and the thin fuzz of black hair at the top of her skinny, parted legs.

'They raped her,' Nairs said in a broken voice, almost as if he were speaking to himself. He pointed to the slimy evidence still visible on her thighs. 'Several of the bastards ... and when they had had their pleasure with her, they murdered her just for pleasure. What ... what a people!'

Nobby squeezed his officer's arm hard. 'She's out of her misery now at least, sir,' he said reassuringly.

Nairs swallowed. 'Yes, you're right.'

'Poor cow,' Nobby agreed. 'Come on, sir. Let's see if those bloody murdering Japs left any grub behind.'

They had. Obviously they had been intent on matters other than food. As they climbed up a rickety ladder to a hut in the centre of the kampong, over the dead body of an old man who had not been quick enough at fleeing as had the rest of the villagers, they could smell the typical odour of pork fat that the Tamils ate with the usual diet of rice and, if they were lucky, chicken. Nobby forgot the cruelly slaughtered pregnant girl in his hunger. 'Come on, sir, that smells like lovely grub.'

It was. Greedily they shoved handfuls of rice and the greasy fat down their throats, washing it down with cool, clean rainwater until replete they lay on their backs on the rattan matting of the place like stranded elephants, barely able to discuss their plans for the morrow. But Nairs forced himself to explain, while at the door, Lee Enfield propped up next to him handily, Nobby listened open-mouthed, his once skinny, but now swollen stomach rumbling loudly.

'Well, this is the picture, as far as I see it,' Nairs said, savouring still the first warm food he had eaten in nearly three days. '*One* – we're on our own. The rest of the patrol must have bumped into Japs – poor devils.'

Nobby nodded his understanding, knowing that the honest little Malays, who would have followed the major to hell and back, wouldn't have survived.

'*Two* – the Japs are still about–'

'Yer – looking for yours truly, the sods.'

'Exactly. *Three* – and this is where it gets tricky. What are they here for? What have the Frogs got to do with them? Why the seaplanes? And what are we supposed to make of that silhouette of a British warship we spotted on that captive Jap we nobbled for a while?'

Nobby nodded sagely and spoiled his wise look a moment later by raising his skinny right haunch and farting pleasurably. He saw the look on Nairs' face in the gloom of the hut and said hastily, 'Had to do it for medical reasons, sir. Might have exploded otherwise.'

Nairs ignored the comment. His mind was racing, trying to make some sense of the whole nasty business. 'A lot of questions, Nobby, but not many answers, eh? But I think we can conclude this. The Japs, using the Frogs as cover, are going to attack

85

Malaya – and attack soon.'

'I'll buy that, sir. Otherwise why are they farting around here where anybody in his right mind wouldn't want to be.'

'But what are they aiming at?' Nairs continued, his long, harshly handsome face creased in a puzzled frown. 'You saw that silhouette of one of our warships. That obviously was important, and where are the Japs going to find Navy battlewagons like that?' Nairs answered his own question. 'You can be sure it isn't in the Gulf of Siam, with enemy-held or pro-enemy territory all around – China, Indo-China and those two-timers, the Siamese. In essence the Japs dominate the South China Sea with their fleet and their air force.'

Nobby wasn't altogether too convinced. He still subscribed to the typical British belief that all Japs were 'four-eyed' and 'couldn't see for toffee apples', as he put it.

Nairs answered his own question when Nobby didn't speak. 'Singapore.'

'Singapore, sir?'

'Yes. It's obvious. Our nearest base to the Japanese at Kota Bharu wouldn't have a chance in hell, if the – we'd better say, *when* the Nips attack Malaya. In fact, they're going to roll up the whole of the Malay peninsula in double-quick time.'

Nobby looked aghast. 'What a grunt-and-grumble, sir. Don't say that, fer God's sake,' he protested.

Nairs shrugged. 'It's my opinion for what it's worth. And I'm going to back it for what it's worth. So, instead of heading for Kota Bharu and the base there, we'll stick to the jungle and head, as originally planned, for Camp Five. I'll tell the Tamils and Malays to make a run for it and then we'll evacuate Susi and the others, heading south all the while. With a bit of luck we'll be able to contact Singapore with our radio from Camp Five and tell 'em we're coming–' The words died on his lips. Suddenly, startlingly, he could see that the little cockney wasn't listening. Instead, his narrow little face tensed and strained, he had cocked his head to one side and was intent on some sound from outside.

'What is it?' Nairs hissed, sitting up straight in alarm and reaching instinctively for his pistol.

'Well, sir,' Nobby whispered, similarly reaching for his rifle, 'by the sound of them plates o' meat out yonder, if ain't no Snowwhite an' her bleeding Seven Dwarves. Them's boots yer can hear, sir – *army boots!*'

Together they squirmed to the open door of the hut on stilts and stared down into the gloom. What they saw at first filled Nairs with renewed hope, but not for long. There were half a dozen giant Sikh police down in the compound, two of them with electric torches which they were flashing to left and right, as if they were searching for something specific. His heart leapt. They were like the Sikhs one saw everywhere in Malaya: immaculately uniformed men, great beards curled outwards under their turbans, armed with their usual long staves to keep order among the native populace.

Now, however, by straining his eyes, he could see that there was something different about this group. First, they were drunk and two of them were carrying rifles instead of the usual lathis. But that wasn't all. They had done something to their khaki uniforms of which they were normally inordinately proud. It wasn't just that the starched shirts and shorts were stained and rumpled, there was something else. All their badges of rank were missing, as were their Indian Army medal ribbons denoting their loyal service to the King-Emperor. They had been ripped off, as had been their epaulettes.

Suddenly it came to Nairs with a flash of

total recall. He had seen Hun soldiers like that just after they had surrendered in France back in 1918. The demoralized German footsloggers had ripped off their medals, too, and had turned their flat caps with the hated insignia of the Hohenzollerns on them inside out as a sign they would serve the Kaiser no longer. It had been the outfit of the typical mutineer. Now it had happened to the Sikhs. They were going over to tomorrow's enemy – the Japs!

Nobby Clark seemed able to read his officer's mind, for he hissed urgently, 'Let's get our arses outa here, sir, before them black heathens shoot 'em off. They've jacked it in.'

The first drunken shot that bored through the straw to the right of the door two foot away confirmed Nobby's conclusion. The Sikhs were working for the Nips now.

Expertly Nobby rolled to one side and in the same movement squeezed off a shot at the Sikhs massing below. There was a cry of rage. A beam of icy light spurted upwards as a policeman flashed on his torch. Nairs didn't wait for them to focus their lights correctly on the exit to the hut on stilts. He loosed off several rapid unaimed shots from his service revolver. There was a yelp of pain and a curse. Another wild shot. Scarlet flame stabbed the growing darkness viciously.

Nairs and Nobby didn't wait for the big bearded cops to correct their aim. As one they rose and slammed into the leaf wall at the far side of the hut. As they expected, it burst immediately with a sharp crack of splintering bamboo supports. 'Jump for it, Nobby!' Nairs yelled above the racket coming from below.

Nobby needed no urging. In the same instant that Nairs flung himself into space, he jumped. He slammed to the ground, happy that he had landed in a heap of shit, carefully collected by the natives for their paddies – at least the noxious stuff had broken his fall. Then, with all confusion, chaos and harsh angry cries from their stalled pursuers, he was running at Nairs' side all out, heading for the cover of the impenetrable mangrove swamps...

Seven

The bosuns' whistles shrilled and the bugles sounded their sweet, silver signals. As the Marines band on the poop deck broke into a lively, happy version of 'A Life on the Ocean Wave', the crowds lining the bank broke into wild cheering, while the civilian craft already anchored off the great port sounded their whistles, the merchant seamen joining in the cheering.

For it was a grand sight to see, and one that Singapore had been waiting for anxiously for over a week now, ever since the rumours of a Japanese declaration of war on the British Empire had commenced circulating in the 'Gibraltar of the East'. Two great Royal Naval ships, one of them the newest addition to the fleet, escorted by four sleek grey destroyers, their crews lining their decks in their immaculately starched whites, with their officers each carrying a gleaming brass-bound telescope under his arm. It was a magnificent display of the power of the British Empire and even the most sceptical of the onlookers that hot, stuffy December day was forced to admit that if anything would put the 'little yellow men' - as they were called superciliously in Singapore – off, it would be this. What could they field to match these symbols of British Imperial might?

The little admiral, dressed in his best starched whites, too, and with the customary telescope beneath his right arm, was not so sanguine. He had heard all the talk about the impregnability of Singapore, especially in the thirties when the government back in Britain had started pumping millions of pounds into the defence of the Far Eastern bastion.

All the same, the many coastal batteries which he could see on both sides of the water had their great gun barrels pointing *out* to sea. What if any attacker – and that attacker could only be the Japs – came from the land? What then? The gun batteries were sited in defence against a landing from the sea – some of them would be as useless as a schoolboy's peashooter. Now he could see why Churchill had taken the risk of sending out the battle wagons to run the dangers of Eastern waters. They were to be Singapore's floating artillery to deter any landward attack. The Great Old Man hoped they would supply the nearest deterrent to stop the Nips attacking. But what if the potential enemy wasn't deterred – *what then?*

It was an overwhelming question that Admiral Sir Tom Phillips was not prepared to answer at that moment of universal joy and excitement. By the time it became acute, it would be too late.

But right through the great modern warship, the matelots had things on their minds at that moment other than the fate of Singapore and the *Prince of Wales* and *Repulse*. Half the ship's company were going be allowed to have twelve hours' liberty on the island. The other half would follow on the morrow. Now, as the ceremonies came to an end, they busied themselves tidying up again for the arrival of the liberty boats, for as Big Slack Arse announced to no one in particular in the crowded mess deck, 'Yer know the frigging Gestapo' – he meant the ship's police – 'they'd stop a bloke from getting rid of his dirty water for having a bit of fluff in his belly button.'

'Dirty water?' the young fair-haired rating they had stopped on the day they had spotted the French sub queried, 'What's that, Stripey?'

'What's that, Stripey?' Big Slack Arse mimicked the young sailor's question in a high falsetto, hand on his hip in a parody of a woman. 'Christ on a crutch, what's the Old Royal coming to? Full of blokes still wet behind the ears.' He grabbed the front of his bell bottoms crudely, 'That's dirty water, sailor and I've got so much o' it, I'll be at it like a fiddler's frigging elbow, as soon as I've handed over my money to one of them Chink bints.' He ended the little diatribe with a contemptuous 'Get some time in, matey.'

Waiting for the launch to take them to Singapore Main HQ, the little admiral, together with Captains Leach and Tennant, who commanded the *Repulse,* watched the happy young men milling around under the hard watchful gaze of the 'Gestapo'. He wondered how many of them would survive the War. Not many he guessed. It hadn't really started yet. Next to him, Tennant, big, bluff and tough, said, 'Most of them are H.O., I suppose, Admiral. But they don't look a bad lot. They've learned a lot since we left Blighty.'

The little admiral was vaguely amused at the *Repulse's* captain's use of 'Blighty'. It dated back to the First World War and showed just how old they really were in comparison to the excited young matelots out to savour the fleshpots of the Far East for the first time and undoubtedly get themselves into trouble in the process in the fashion of sailors ever since Nelson's time. 'Yes, Bill, they have. All the same we've got to look after 'em the best we can. They're some mothers' sons, after all, aren't they?'

Tennant looked at his superior officer out of the corner of his eye, wondering a little at the little admiral's comment and the manner in which he expressed it. But he kept his thoughts to himself, contenting himself with remarking, 'We'll do our best, Admiral.'

Half an hour later, introductions completed, a glass of good Chinese beer hastily down, they sat down in Naval and Army Combined HQ to receive the latest briefing on the situation in the Far East. And the importance the Governor placed on this first encounter between the base officers and the new arrivals was emphasized by the fact that no less a person than the C-in-C, Lieutenant-General Percival, himself gave it.

Not that the little admiral was impressed

by the army man. He knew that Percival was nicknamed the 'chinless wonder' behind his back and he looked it. Just underneath his trim little moustache, his jaw seemed to disappear so that he seemed to possess no jaw at all. But like so many weak looking men, in the Admiral's experience, he was stubborn, self-opinionated and very definitely self-satisfied, as if he, personally, could never do anything wrong; that would be the fault of others.

Bored at the general's long lecture on the firepower of the port's guns and the effectiveness of the shore batteries, the little admiral looked out of the large window at the street below. It was crowded with large imported American touring cars and was filled with well-dressed men and women who looked as if they didn't have a care in the world. He knew that this night the clubs, the hotels, the night clubs would be crowded with tuxedo-clad men from 'up country' and their wives – or whores bare-shouldered and bejewelled, who continued to live their ostrich-like life here in Singapore. They had seen the newsreels of the 'war back home' – Dunkirk, the bombing, the surrender of France and the like – but all of them, the admiral knew, were convinced that it 'can't happen here.'

Percival, with his rabbit's teeth and pop eyes, seemed to share that feeling. 'Personally, gentlemen,' he concluded the boring lecture to the assembled naval brass, 'I am all for letting the little yellow men attack.' He beamed at them, his prominent Adam's apple sliding up and down his scraggy neck like an express lift in one of Singapore's fancy new skyscrapers. 'Then we'll show the world. We'll give the buggers a real bloody nose. Thank you.' He paused, almost as if he expected applause. Then he sat down, his rabbit's face still set in an inane smile.

'And what if the Japs don't attack from the sea, which you expect them to do?' the little admiral asked, trying to take the general down a peg or two. But before Percival could answer, he snapped swiftly, 'Better not try to answer that, General, I know what you will say. Instead, let me ask you and your gentlemen from intelligence this.' He looked at the red-tabbed staff officers sitting behind their commander, looking as wooden and as hidebound as he did. 'What is a French sub doing helping the Japanese? A Japanese soldier, too, by all appearance?' He paused and added, 'You got my signal on the matter, didn't you?'

Percival nodded. He looked at his Chief of Intelligence, a middle-aged, paunchy colonel, his chest ablaze with medal ribbons. He rose and addressed the sailors, 'Gentlemen, we have no explanation for the presence of the Frogs with the Jap officer.' He pulled a face suddenly, as if he had smelled something decidedly unpleasant right underneath his red, bulbous, drinker's nose. 'But we all know the Frogs from the last show. Decidedly unsteady. What can you expect from men who make love with their tongues, what?' He beamed at them, willing them to laugh at the crudity of his supposed joke. The naval men didn't oblige him. Instead, at a nod from their admiral, they reached for their caps. Sir Tom said, 'I shall be submitting you a detailed plan of my intentions for the next seventy-two hours, General,' he said, addressing the C-in-C. 'It will probably entail that we sail once more by that time. I hope I can rely on your staff to help me with supply problems?'

'Of course, of course,' Percival agreed hastily, showing that mouthful of protruding rabbit's teeth of his. 'But I wouldn't be too hasty to leave Singapore.'

The little admiral didn't comment.

Instead he nodded in a perfunctory way, but outside in the staff car once more, he exploded to Captain Leach, 'God on High, John, does that buggering, chinless wonder know there's a war on?' He sighed a little helplessly. 'What is it that poet chappie, Eliot, says?'

Leach looked back at him a little helplessly as they headed, with much hornblowing, for the Governor's Residency to make their courtesy call – naval officers were not given much to reading modern poetry. He, personally, had never advanced any further than Kipling, and Rupert Brooke and his 'foreign field' stuff.

'I'll tell you, John. He said something about the world ending not with a bang but with a whimper. Well, he'd be wrong here.'

'What do you mean sir?'

'I'll not draw you a picture,' the admiral replied. 'But this damned, *too* comfortable place, is not ending with a whimper. It'll go with one hell of a bang – and with it,' his blue eyes bored into Leach's surprised face for a moment, 'will go the British Empire as well...' He breathed out hard as if he were exasperated beyond all measure. 'I've no claims to being a damned prophet, John, but the fall of Singapore will be a signal. You

99

just wait and see.' Suddenly, startlingly, he clapped his mouth closed like some irate reader might a book that he could no longer read and lapsed into silence

Next to him Leach did the same. All the same his mind was racing as he pondered 'Tom Thumb's' words. Suddenly he felt a cold finger of fear trace its slow way down his spine and he knew he and the rest were doomed.

And all over Singapore, while the great and the good – and the not so good – enjoyed themselves in fancy hotels and bars, and the young matelots paid their handfuls of hot coins for the tawdry favours of the cheap whores of every colour and sexual perversion, the little unseen Japanese, bespectacled and always smiling in their humble manner, hurried back and forth through the brothels, the pleasure gardens, the stores, the docks, their quick, dark eyes noting the information needed so urgently in faraway Tokyo now that the Military had made their decision.

It wouldn't be long now...

It was Saturday, 1 December 1941.

Book Two: Raise The Alarm

One

It was nearly dawn now. Already the dirty white sky was beginning to flush a faded pink. Soon it would be daylight, a transformation which would take place with the startling suddenness of the tropics. But the two weary unshaven men, their uniforms already ragged from the thorns and barbs of the thick jungle they had fought their way through that night, had no eyes for the beauties of the approaching dawn. Besides, they were already concerned with the possible dangers of the new day.

It had been a night of alarms and near escapes. At first, they had stuck to the orderly lines of rubber trees which lay to both sides of the single black road leading south. It had been the easiest way to make quick progress. But soon after the first burst of excited firing out of what seemed nowhere, they had headed for the confines and cover of the jungle.

They had been just in time. From then onwards it seemed that they heard and occasionally glimpsed what they took to be enemy parties for the rest of the night.

Even the night animals had stilled at the sudden bursts of automatic fire, the whoosh of signal rockets and the cries, enraged or inquiring, in a couple of tongues, one of which was completely foreign to Nairs and Nobby Clark.

'It's not the Tamils,' Nobby had commented. 'Besides, those poor buggers, with not a pot to piss in are shit-scared of the darkness. Who could the dirty sods be?'

Grimly Major Nairs had answered the little cockney's question to the best of his ability. 'Japs – and probably those Sikhs who seem to be helping the little yellow men.'

'But we're not at war with 'em – *yet.*' Nobby had objected, as they had fought their way ever deeper into the mangroves and bamboo of the jungle once again, the sweat and the midges, which were everywhere, blinding them.

'Don't matter to the Nips,' Nairs had gasped, lashing out with his parang. 'The last time they went to war, with the Russians back in oh-five, they just attacked and declared war afterwards.'

'But what have the frigging Sikhs to do with them, sir?'

'The Japs have been going on about their bloody Co-Prosperity Sphere for years. Tremendous propaganda. Appeals to simple folk. Kick out the whites and we Asiatic folk will inherit the world. Sweetness and light all the way. The Sikhs have bought it. The Malays will in due course. Perhaps even the poor down-trodden Tamils. In the end the only people we'll be able to trust will be the Chinks because they've been fighting the Japs for nearly a decade as it is. Now put a sock in it, Nobby, and let's get deeper into this bloody jungle.'

That had been what seemed now an age before. Now the jungle was silent save for the noises monkeys made at dawn and the calls of the birds. So there they slumped, munching the bitter black chocolate of their emergency ration, squatting in the cover of big juicy ferns six foot in height. They weren't hungry, but Nairs had given the official order* to break into the two tins of

*Footnote on next page.

chocolate, because as he told Nobby, 'We need the energy, old chap.'

To which Nobby had replied miserably, 'What I need, sir, is a nice pint of wallop, a dusky maiden and then a quick posting to the Army Postal Corps in – say – Bognor Regis.'

Nairs had been too tired and worried to laugh. But after he had eaten the chocolate and had felt new energy surging through his body from the sugar, he had risen, slit open one of the fat pulpy ferns and had drunk the slightly bitter water that came from the cut greedily. As he did so, he told himself that as long as they had water they'd be all right. They could go a long way without food.

After Nobby had done the same, he had allowed him to light up and smoke, reasoning the smell of European cigarette smoke would be covered almost immediately by the fresh dampness of the new dawn and not give their presence away to any enemy scout in the near.

'All right, Nobby listen to this,' he commanded.

*An officer had to give an order to open the brass-bound tin of chocolate. It was a punishable offence for a private soldier to do so without permission.

'I'm all ears,' Nobby answered brightly, expecting the usual answer.

Nairs didn't give it. Things were too urgent and too serious for 'wisecracks', as the Yanks called them. Instead, he cleared the jungle floor in front of them, sending the ants that were everywhere scuttling for cover and drew two parallel lines in the damp earth. 'To the left, the Gulf of Siam. To the right – roughly – the route of march we're following. Got it?'

Nobby nodded, but said nothing.

'Here to the left, Kuala Lumpur,' he made a dot with the point of the twig and then another. 'Here – our objective – Camp Five.'

'England, Home and Beauty,' Nobby said a little dreamily, apropos of nothing.

'If you like. Now I reckon we've got another four hours' march – I think we can manage it in that time even in this bloody jungle – before we reach Camp Five. Then–'

'That is if the Nips and their ruddy Sikhs don't get onto us first, sir,' Nobby interrupted.

'Agreed,' Nairs said. 'But my guess is they'll be sticking to the coast because they're going to land there sooner or later –and I fear that will be sooner.' Abruptly the Major looked very worried, and Nobby knew why. It wasn't just a Jap invasion that concerned his old boss, it was his wife, Susi. The Japs hated Eurasians who married white men with great passion. He didn't know why except that the handful of Japs he had got to know in the past had had this racial thing about the purity of Jap blood. If the Japs reached Camp Five before they did and got Susi and the rest away, the boss's beautiful half-Malay wife wouldn't live long.

'There's another thing, too,' Nairs continued as above the dirty-white, red-streaked, pre-dawn sky gave way to blue, and on the horizon the sun rose like a glowing blood-red ball. 'I've been thinking about that silhouette we spotted on the Jap prisoner back on the coast and wondering what ship it was.'

'Well, it was certainly no Jap, sir,' Nobby said firmly. 'You can tell their navy ships right off. They're bent in the bloody middle as if they're going sink at any bloody minute and they've got them bridges that look like a bloody Wog pagoda.'

'Exactly. That was a British ship all right and do you know which?'

'Search me, sir,' Nobby answered, dimly becoming aware of the noises a long way off.

'I think it's one of the new *George V* class. They started laying them down at the start of the War. I suppose Whitehall thought they were going to be the only ships in the Royal Navy capable of tackling the Jerry pocket battleships and the like.'

'I remember now, sir. I was in England in thirty-nine on my bi-annual leave when they laid down the keel of one of them – the *Prince of Wales*, if I remember correct like.' His frowned deepened. There definitely was somebody out there.

'So what do you make of it?' Nairs asked, apparently unaware of the noises.

'Leave the thinking, sir, to the officers and gentlemen,' Nobby tried to deflect his rising inner tension. 'They get paid for it.'

Nairs gave him a wintry grin, though he was in no mood for humour. Naturally he had heard the noises, too, and the faint baying of the dogs that went with them. 'Cheeky beggar,' he declared and then went on hastily. 'Let's get it together, Nobby. The Frogs and their seaplanes; the Japs with the Frogs and what looks like the wholesale desertion of the Sikh police, who always know things more quickly than we do. The Asiatic grapevine, I suppose.'

'Bleeding wogs,' Nobby grunted, typical

Englishman that he was. He always maintained that there was nothing like an Englishman or England, though Nairs often thought that the 'Old Country', as Nobby called it, had done precious little for the latter: council school, a slum, bread and dripping for most meals washed down with stewings of old tea leaves and then the Great War. It was only since he had followed Nairs to Malaya that he had worn a suit that had not come from the 'pop shop'.*

'Yes, of course, *bleeding wogs*,' Nairs humoured the little man, who in another age had won the Military Medal for having carrying a wounded Punjabi infantryman back to their own lines under intense Turkish fire in Palestine. 'But let's get on while we've still got time. It's obvious the Japs are about to invade us in force. This is just an armed recce. Their objective will be Singapore naturally – and the only way that the powers-that-be can save that Imperial white elephant is to nip the Jap invasion in the bud when it comes ... And how can they do that?' He paused, let his words sink in and then answered his own question. 'I'll tell you. They'll have to send the Royal Navy

*Pawn shop.

to deal with the Jap seaborne invasion. But the Japs, if they know that – and I suspect the cunning bastards do – won't want to show their hand too early. They won't want their troop transports caught out offshore by powerful British warships. And that's where the Frogs come in, neutral as they're supposed to be–'

'You mean,' Nobby snapped, for despite his protestations that thinking had to be left to 'officers and gents', he had a very sharp mind, 'let the Frogs spot our fleet, inform the Japs in advance and then the Japs can engage our boys in blue while the foot-sloggers set about their invasion without interference?'

'Something of that nature.'

'But if the Royal Navy doesn't know what's going on up here, their ships might just walk into a trap, with the Jap Navy waiting to blow the living daylights outa 'em.'

'Not the Jap *Navy*,' Nairs corrected him, 'but the Jap *Air Force!*'

Nobby Clark's mouth dropped open. After a minute he breathed, 'Get you, sir. We ain't got the planes out here to tackle the Jap fighters and bombers. They've gone to Blighty and the Middle East. All Singapore's got left is a lot of old crates from before the War, flying on a wing and a prayer, made of orange boxes and old women's silk drawers.'

'Something like that, Nobby,' Nairs mused, realizing of course that Nobby was right; and for the first time he saw the full enormity of the situation. If the Royal Navy was not warned, their ships would sail right into a bloody trap once the balloon went up just as the Russian fleet had done back in 1905. It had moved into the unknown and had been destroyed almost completely by the waiting Japs, leaving Russia's land troops completely at the mercy of the Imperial Army. Suddenly he was overcome by a great sense of urgency that drove away all weariness.

Ignoring his stiff bones, he rose to his feet and hitched his pistol belt higher. 'Come on,' he ordered. 'Digit out of the orifice – get yer finger out.'

'Have a heart, sir,' Nobby mumbled, but he rose willingly enough, slinging the heavy rifle as he did so.

Nairs didn't even answer. Not waiting to see if his old running mate was following, he raised his parang and started slashing the tough bamboo canes with renewed energy.

Behind him Nobby sighed, 'Heaven help a frigging sailor on a night like this,' and followed.

To their rear the baying of the hounds and the sound of angry voices grew louder...

Two

Colonel Moto raised his sword, looking to left and right as if he were some general in a heroic nineteenth-century Japanese picture ordering his army into a great battle. To his left and right, the Imperial Guardsmen, giants all, tensed over their bayoneted rifles. In front of them the skirmish line of turbaned Sikhs did the same. They were giants, too, but they had no intention of dying for the Imperial Ruler in Tokyo if they could help it; they were here for the plunder, loot and because they wanted to be on the winning side.

To their front, the plantation compound went about its morning business unaware of what was going to happen to it in a few minutes. The elephants used for drawing out the heavy timber were snorting and trumpeting in that early morning bad-tempered fashion of theirs. Women, bare-foot for the most part were moving back and forth, bearing jugs on their heads or carrying piles of chapattis wrapped in leaves for their labourer husbands. Tamils squatted on their skinny haunches waiting for the day's work to commence, spitting and hawking into the dust, or chewing stolidly on brick-red betel nut. It was the age-old scene of a village community in the Asia at the break of another boiling-hot working day.

Colonel Moto had no eyes for such matters. He saw the tumbledown kampong strictly with military eyes – best field of fire, need for flanking attack to left and right, areas of dead ground, etc. In this case, his main aim was to take the place with as little loss as possible and, more importantly, ensure that no one escaped. It was still several days before the main Imperial attack would come in on the coast to his rear. He didn't want to alert the damned devil dogs of round eyes before then.

His mind was made up, knowing that if there were any armed defenders down there, they would be partially blinded firing into the rising sun. That thought pleased him. It reminded him of the great warrior nation to which he belonged. He raised his treasured family Samurai sword and cried proudly at the top of his voice. *'Banzai!'*

'Banzai,' the Imperial Guardsmen echoed

in a great throaty bass as down below the half-starved dogs began to bark in protest and the skinny chickens scattered wildly. Then they were advancing, the Sikhs in front, the guardsmen at their slow, measured pace, the sun's rays gleaming silver off their long bayonets.

Below, panic broke out as the barefoot natives saw this line of steel advancing on them. Native women grabbed their naked, fat-bellied babies. A Tamil cook overturned a great steaming cauldron of polished rice in haste to get away from the approaching danger. Suddenly all was chaos and confusion, with natives running back and forth grabbing their pathetic bits and pieces, screaming and shrieking, as they lost their heads wondering what to do; while in the bungalow, which Moto knew must house the round-eyed plantation bosses, a lone rifle took up the challenge, with single shots potting the ranks of the Sikhs.

But the renegade police were taken up by the wild atavistic fury of battle. They charged forward at the double, armed mostly just with their leaded bamboo stakes. Here and there a man went down, whirled round by the impact of a bullet at such close range. Another simply lowered himself to the dust of the compound and stared at his shattered guts, as if unable to understand what had caused this snake-like steaming grey length of guts to begin protruding from the great, red, gory hole of his stomach.

Moto advancing, dark eyes flashing excitedly behind the line of giant guardsmen, blew a shrill blast on his whistle. 'At the double now!' he yelled hoarsely, carried away by the almost sexual excitement of the attack. The guardsmen needed no urging. Their blood was up. They were imbued by that overwhelming, primeval desire to kill. They hurried for-ward, crying the unintelligible obscenities and curses of crazy men.

At the lower right window of the bungalow, the lone man redoubled his fire. A guardsman came to an abrupt halt. The rifle fell from his suddenly nerveless fingers. He stood there for what seemed an age. His hands clawed the air as if he were climbing the rungs of an invisible ladder. He was, it appeared to Moto, attempting to fight off death, remaining on his feet, dying by the second as he did so. Then, with soft groan as if with despair, he pitched face-forward, dead before he hit the dirt.

That did it. The guardsmen gave up all

attempts to maintain their line. They dashed forward, bayonets flashing in the sun. They hurried in and out of the huts, slashing, stabbing, chopping. Natives went down on all sides, men, women and children. They showed no mercy. Everything that came before those crimson-tipped blades *had* to die.

Coming up to the side of the bungalow, Moto saw that the lone defender was still firing, picking off the attackers coolly and calmly, making every shot count, as if he were back on some peacetime range and had all the time in the world to ensure he struck the bull every time.

Moto caught his breath and turned the sweat-lathered hilt of the curved Samurai sword to get a better hold of it now that he was going in for the final kill. He counted to three, trying to compose himself. All around him there were wild cries of battle. They receded into the distance. Then his booted foot lashed out and smashed against the flimsy door which flew open. He dashed inside, wielding his great sword, slashing and whirling it from side to side in the manner that his fencing master had taught him all those years before. He took in the scene immediately.

At the far end of the room, a half-naked young woman was crouched over an old-fashioned radio transmitter, trying frantically to make it work, spinning the dials, pulling out the levers. Next to the woman, a turbaned native, grey-bearded and determined, was crouched firing out of the window, surrounded by gleaming empty cartridge cases and boxes of ammunition.

Moto let out a great and frightening yell. The woman screamed and turned. His eyes fell on her plump naked young breasts. But there was no time for *that* yet. His sword cleaved through the air and shattered the aerial on top of the set. The woman tumbled crazily from her chair, her legs spread as she tried to break her fall. He caught a glimpse of her naked, shaven, powdered pubes as he stepped over her and aimed a blow at the Indian.

The man was old but he was quick. He knew he couldn't fire without hitting the screaming Eurasian woman. Instead, he parried the blow with his rifle. Moto felt a stinging electric shock race through his sword arm but ignored it. He swung again, eyes popping out of his head with rage that this contemptible native should attempt to stop him – a Japanese colonel! His blow struck home. The Indian dropped his rifle. Blood spurting a scarlet jet from where the fingers of his right hand had just been.

'Go!' he shouted at the woman in English. 'Go!'

But she was too terrified to move, as the Indian, dripping blood as he did so, backed off, his old rheumy eyes still defiant despite his wound. He spat on the floor in front of the advancing Colonel Moto, sword upraised for the kill. It was a deliberate insult and Moto knew it. He was trying to give the panic-stricken woman time to escape. 'Come, chicken,' Moto called softly in Japanese, beckoning to the Indian with his hand momentarily, 'come and be slaughtered!' It was as if he were tempting the wounded Indian to come forward and be killed. But Nairs' old bearer, a veteran of France and the NorthWest Frontier, wasn't to be taken that easily. He pretended to look down at his wounded hand so that Moto could not see the look in his old eyes.

Moto was caught off-guard and relaxed momentarily. The old bearer didn't give him a second chance. He flung himself forward with the last of his strength and slammed into the surprised Moto, whose sword tumbled from his hand. The bearer cried,

'Come on, Missy, *run for it.*'

Next moment he had thrown himself into the little vegetable yard outside and was running the best he could, with his wounded hand dripping scarlet blood behind him into the ground, for the cover of the jungle. Behind him he left a winded Moto glaring at the half-naked girl who had failed to follow the bearer's command. In her turn she stared back at the Japanese officer crouching on one knee on the floor, mesmerized with fear, waiting like a dumb animal for the terrible fate that the Japanese had in store for her...

'*Oh my God!*' Nairs had cried from the depths of his suddenly anguished being. '*It's the Camp... My Susi!*' Immediately, without waiting for Nobby's reaction, he had set off running, blindly blundering through the jungle, ignoring the barbed fronds whipping and lashing his tormented face.

'*Sir!*' Nobby had tried to warn him, but the cry had died on his lips. He knew Nairs wasn't listening. Now, his chest heaving, his arms working back and forth like pistons, he followed Nairs, heading in the direction of the firefight, knowing even as he did so that they would arrive too late. All that Camp

119

Five had to defend itself now, with Nairs' Malay Scouts gone, was Guptha – one lone veteran, long past his prime, armed with an antiquated rifle that Nobby thought probably dated back to the turn of the century.

Still they blundered on through the thick jungle, all care thrown to the wind, ignoring the bloody buffeting that the creepers and thorns were inflicting upon them with such cruelty. Nobby knew why. Susi was pregnant. 'Three months gone!' Nairs had exclaimed joyfully to Nobby just before they had left on that fateful patrol in what now seemed another age.

'In the pudding club ... at your age, sir,' he had attempted to pull the officer's leg. 'Bit naughty, if I may say so.'

But Nairs had been too enthralled by the news given him by a blushing Susi to notice, as the three of them had stood there, so taken up by the exciting disclosure that they didn't even notice the tom-tom beat of the moonsoon rain on the tin roof above them.

Now Nairs, like a man demented, bulled his way through the jungle, as if he already knew the danger his wife was in; that every minute counted. But Fate was against him. Abruptly he was stopped in his tracks by a low, threatening, throaty growl which they had heard before. The two of them stopped at once, their skinny chests heaving frantically.

A large yellow dog had emerged slowly from the jungle. It half crouched, eyeing them menacingly, its ugly yellow teeth bared, the saliva dripping down the sides of its massive jaws, the muscles rippling the length of its body. 'I'll be buggered,' Nobby said with mock bravado, 'the frigging hound of the Baskervilles–' His voice died away immediately as the great killer dog turned its head in his direction and gave another growl. It seemed to a suddenly petrified Nobby that the hound was marking him down for his next snack. His knees started to tremble uncontrollably.

Nairs stood there in an agony of suspense, trying to outguess the hound which barred their way. He knew the type. They were a specially bred dog from Japan's northern islands, used for guard duties in all sorts of weather, replacing men, too, when they were employed in carrying military supplies and, on occasion, to run through minefields to clear a path for the follow-up infantry. Nothing could stop them – they were tremendously strong and ferocious – save death itself. What was he going to do?

Slowly, infinitely slowly, he crouched low, the dog watching him suspiciously all the time, ready to spring at him at a moment's notice.

Behind his OC Nobby knew instinctively what Nairs was going to do. He said a speedy prayer that he would be able to pull it off. Reaching out behind him so that the dog couldn't see the movement, he sought and found the stone they would need.

'Got it, sir,' he croaked, hardly recognizing his own voice.

Nairs didn't answer – he didn't want to do anything that might deflect the killer dog from him. He waited, crouched, trying to assess how the beast would move when he gave his command. Now all was silent to their front save a faint, hardly audible screaming. He winced. He knew instinctively what was now happening at Camp Five. Time was running out – *fast!*

The dog had begun to crouch. The muscles in its back legs were tensed, rippling back and forth under the tight skin. Its ears had flattened the length of its head, teeth bared even wider, its breath coming in sharp harsh gasps through distended nostrils. Nairs knew what that meant. The hound was about to spring at him. He knew he couldn't let that happen. Even if he could ward the beast off, the racket the hunting dog would make would bring its handler and the rest of their pursuers running. It was now or never.

'Throw, Nobby!' he commanded in a harsh gasp.

The little cockney didn't hesitate. He whipped the stone over his head as if he were lobbing a grenade into the dense bushes to his right. Instinctively the hound swung its sloping head in that direction. Nairs dived forward and with one hand he grabbed for the animal's tightly strung testicles; with the other he sought blindly for its muzzle.

The beast's howl of pain was muffled as he pressed hard. It writhed, twisting its head back and forth, trying to avoid the other hand, digging its hindlegs in as he grasped for the muzzle, trying to throw off that cruel grip.

It ripped its claws savagely across Nairs' crimson-stained face. He yelped with agony as they tore the flesh, and blood started to spurt out. Behind him, Nobby had risen to his feet. Wildly, hopping back and forth like a crazy schoolboy playing hop-scotch, he tried to bring the brass butt of his rifle down onto the dog's head – to no avail. In its mortal agony, the dog dodged his frenzied blows time and time again ... and in the distance came the sound of running feet, curses and the thwack and cut of someone cutting through the bamboo at a tremendous rate. *The Japs were coming...*

Three

The Tamil girl screamed shrilly as an Imperial guardsman lowered himself onto her naked body. There were four others holding her down. She couldn't have been more than twelve. Her breasts were non-existent and there was the merest brown fluff at her stomach where the two guardsmen holding her, red-faced and drunk on looted whisky, had spread her skinny kid's legs as far as they would open for their comrade. Now he, his breeches hanging around his put-tees, was trying to penetrate her, as she wriggled back and forth desperately, sobbing all the while as she did so.

Moto savoured the sight. But it wasn't the rape of the little girl which entranced him – it was the impression it made on the half-naked Eurasian whore, with her distorted face and arms akimbo, trying to hide her full breasts from the grinning, drunken soldiers' gaze. She knew what was coming all right, Colonel Moto told himself. She'd better prepare for it. In the end, he knew, she'd like it, beg him to continue, stick it ever deeper into her delightful secret place. If she didn't ... well, it would end that way, anyhow. They had no time to take prisoners, even if they were as beautiful and desirable as the Eurasian whore.

The guardsman finally found what he sought. He thrust home his loins. The girl's naked body arched like a taut bow as she screamed. The guardsman showed no mercy as he thrust home harder. The girl's eyes seemed about to pop from her head. Froth splattered from her gaping mouth as the guardsman, grunting like a pig now, started to pump himself in and out of her transfixed body, while the others holding the tormented girl cheered him on.

Colonel Moto took his eyes off the victim and flashed another look at Susi. She was sobbing openly now, hands fallen to her sides, not caring that she was revealing those delightful breasts to anyone who cared to look. Moto wanted more, but he knew to achieve his purpose he needed the stimulus of the tortured girl. Now, as the guardsman, gasping like someone who had just run a great race, almost achieved his final purpose, his comrades relaxed their hold –

their help was no longer needed now – and were ripping open their own flies. They were going to have their turn with her, too.

The thought excited Colonel Moto beyond measure. He felt his own breath coming in short, sharp gasps so it hurt. He swayed as if he might fall. He was dizzy with lust. She would be easy, he told himself, the words, even as he thought them, coming in short disjointed jerks. She would not object. How could she? The knowledge excited him even more. He felt he must choke if he didn't have her soon – NOW!

Now the first guardsman had entered the bloody victim of the rape attack. The man was gasping like an ancient asthmatic in the throes of his last attack. His skinny buttocks were pumping up and down, while next to him, the second candidate stood trembling, ready to take his place.

Colonel Moto could wait no longer. He strode to the crying Eurasian and grabbed her breasts roughly in his big hands. Face contorted, livid almost as if he were consumed by a terrible rage, he gasped in Japanese, 'Come ... fuck ... fuck!' He pushed her and tried to knock her onto her back. Suddenly she reacted and raked his face with her long sharp nails.

He jerked back, the hot blood dripping down the side of his yellow face. 'Whore!' he exclaimed. For a moment he was tempted to reach for his sword and teach her a lesson. The sharp point of the centuries-old Samurai blade would soon put an end to the prettiness of her face. But no, he would enjoy her first and teach her what a real Asiatic man was like after those weak, effete round eyes to whom she had sold herself for money.

He planted his lips on hers and cruelly bit her. She writhed and screamed as he laughed thickly. He felt himself getting hard at the thought of the indignities he would now inflict upon her naked, nubile, dark body. While he held her down thus with his weight, his greedy fingers felt the length of her body and found that source of all delight.

He grunted pleasurably. 'Now,' he cried. 'Now you shall have it – and enjoy–' The words died on his thick lips as from outside there came the sudden burst of rifle fire, followed by cries of alarm in Japanese.

His erection vanished at once. He levered himself up from her, unable for a moment to grasp what was happening. 'Stand to!' the sentries he had posted at the edge of the kampong called out. A Sikh policeman carrying a struggling, looted goat stopped suddenly, a stupid grin spreading over his broad, bearded face. The goat slipped from his abruptly sagging shoulders and ran off madly. Next moment the Sikh dropped dead.

Now there seemed to be wild firing coming from all sides. Moto cursed. He pulled his flies together, seizing his sword at the same time. On the table, the bloody girl, her lips already swollen from his cruel bites, fell back and started to sob bitterly.

Moto forgot her for the moment. He had caught a glimpse of a white face and figure slipping through the jungle to the right of the bungalow. Instinctively he knew to whom the figure belonged – one of the round eyes they had been searching for. He slapped the guardsman nearest him, who was still fumbling stupidly with his flies after taking his turn with the native child. 'There, you great oaf,' he cried frantically. 'Over there – shoot him with your damned rifle, man!' Exasperated beyond all measure, he reached up and slapped the guardsman across the face viciously in the fashion of the Japanese Army.*

*Footnote on next page.

129

The guardsman collected himself. Hurriedly he grabbed and aimed at the spot, but the rifle only clicked. He had forgotten to take off his safety catch! When he had done so and aimed again, the figure had gone. But still from the outside of the compound some hidden figure was maintaining accurate and rapid fire on the area surrounding the bungalow, as if in an attempt to isolate it and the men inside the place from the rest.

Moto guessed this meant that an attack was being launched on the bungalow itself. 'All right ... leave the women,' he cried above the snap and crackle of rifle fire, the bleat and cackle of the frightened goats and poultry and the enraged, bewildered cries of the Sikhs who had gone to ground and were blazing away, without aim, in all directions. 'Prepare for an assault. Come on, now. Pre-

*In the old Imperial Japanese Army, when an officer slapped a sergeant for some misdemeanour, the latter would slap his corporal; the corporal, in his turn, would slap the next closest rank and so on right down to the humble private. It was thought by the Japanese that this was the best way of maintaining discipline in a mainly peasant army.

pare for an assault!'

Cursing madly, the sweat drops dripping down his furrowed brow, Nobby blazed away like he had done that terrible dawn back in March 1918 when the whole German Imperial Army had attacked out of the mist and he and his pals had thought all of that millions-strong Army were coming their way personally. All the same, he kept an eye on the dwindling pile of rounds which he had taken from his last bandolier of ammunition and placed at his side in the grass. He had a splendid position on a piece of high ground overlooking the kampong so that he could dominate the whole place as long as the still confused Japs didn't organize and rush him from several different directions. That would mean curtains. Yer, a harsh little cynical voice rasped at the back of his mind, and if the Old Man doesn't get finished soon, your frigging number'll be up. For he knew he probably only had enough cartridges to keep on firing at this rate for another few minutes. A Sikh tried to rise to his feet, clutching his long bamboo stave, with which in peacetime the Sikh had used to beat the heads in of stubborn peasants. Nobby Clark didn't even seem to aim. He tucked his rifle butt into his skinny shoulder more firmly and fired in one and the same movement. The Sikh came to an abrupt stop, his massive legs giving beneath him like those of a new-born foal. He went down in an instant, and Nobby remarked, with more confidence than he felt, 'And another pesky Redskin went and bit the dust.'

A hundred yards away, Nairs skirted the back of the bungalow, body crouched low, revolver fully loaded. There was the sound of firing from his old home, but it was coming from the front windows and the veranda and he guessed they hadn't spotted his flanking tactic yet. He sped a silent prayer heavenwards that the Japs wouldn't until he'd rescued Susi. He continued his silent progress, his boots wreathed in dust, his heart beating furiously. But he had been through this sort of thing often enough before. Once the moment of truth arrived, he told himself confidently, that instant when he would launch himself into the attack, he would be ice-cold, all fear and apprehension vanished.

He grew ever closer to the rear of the bungalow and spotted Susi's vegetable garden where she had tried – and failed – to raise the kind of greens that she thought the

English ate all the time, including Brussels sprouts, which Nairs hated. He squirmed his way through the giant overgrown shoots which had dwarfed Susi when she had worked in the garden, not taking his gaze off the bungalow for an instant. As he moved, he planned where he'd break in. Not through a window. That would make a racket, he might cut himself seriously and he didn't want any loss of blood now. The kitchen was out too. For all he knew the Jap swine and their treacherous helpers might be looting the place at this very moment. It would have to be one of the bedrooms. Not Susi's though. Looters, he knew from past experience, always took their time rifling through women's drawers and things. He supposed it was something vaguely sexual. No, it would be his own bedroom. There was nothing of value there, save a cup he had won in 1917 just as he had left school for his commission, and a few surviving yellowing photographs of the intervening years. Not even the Japs would be interested in him posing with a hunting rifle and one foot placed triumphantly on the massive head of a dead rogue water buffalo which had plagued the natives back in the late twenties when he had been full of youthful

133

'piss and vinegar' and had delighted in the killing of God's creatures.

The thought reminded him. Now he was going to kill, not wild animals but something more dangerous and deadly – armed wild men. He swallowed hard and tensed at the blind to his bedroom. Cautiously he reached in a hand through the air gap below and infinitely slowly, taking care not to make the slightest sound – though the Japs were still blazing away furiously at nothing – he raised the blind. Next moment, holding it there awkwardly, he slipped inside and smelled the old familiar odour of his bedroom – whisky, violet hair pomade, polished native furniture. Instinctively he looked at the group photo of the young soldiers some- where outside Etaples in France where they had been prepared for shipment to the trenches. How young and confident they all looked, with some of them, strictly contradictory to King Regulations, wearing their old school scarves around their necks – there was even one carrying a tennis racket!

He frowned. Hardly one of them had been alive six months later: all the rest had been devoured by the greedy, insatiable maws of the God of War. But the thought made him even more determined. *They* had fought to defend right against wrong and died doing so. Now he was doing the same, fighting the same beast in a different guise on the other side of the world. He couldn't let them down. They deserved the best he could give: those youths with their silly pretensions – old school ties, affected drawls, sporting gear – who had died young even before they had begun to live. He gripped his weapon more firmly, harshly handsome face set and determined. Just as they had when they had been about to go over the top waiting for the company commander on the 'stoop' to blow his whistle which would begin that terrible match with death, he started to count off the seconds, *'ONE ... TWO...'*

Four

Admiral Phillips stood in the middle of the ward-room which still smelled of fresh paint and new leather from the couches and easy chairs that were everywhere, and surveyed his officers and those from the *Repulse* and the destroyers. He had ordered them all here so that even the most junior 'snotty' would know what was going on. After this they would be venturing into the unknown, without the kind of support they would normally receive in Home Waters or even the Med. Who knew what task might fall to them? It was better that they were all prepared for every eventuality.

He let them sip their only drink – as usual it was pink gin, not 'grog' or rum as the general public always supposed Navy men drank – and told himself they were a good-looking bunch. They were men – and even boys in the shape of the cadets – who he could rely upon. All the same, the knowledge that they were so dependable weighed him down somewhat. It made him

136

even more conscious of his responsibility to each and every one of them – old hand and boy straight from Dartmouth and wet behind the ears.

Finally, after the Captain of Marines had entered the wardroom and whispered discreetly, 'All bumboats and the like cleared away, sir. Guard mounted,' indicating that the *Prince of Wales* was sealed off against prying eyes and too big ears, he nodded to a waiting Tennant.

Tennant drained the rest of his glass in one go and, tapping on a silver wardroom tray, the Captain of the *Repulse* said in a loud voice that often enough had carried over a Force Twelve gale, 'Gentlemen, may I have your attention. The Admiral would like to speak to you.'

A few coughs and they were ready and expectant, looking at him like a bunch of open-mouthed schoolkids at a birthday party waiting for the conjuror to produce a rabbit out of his silk hat. The admiral smiled softly at the thought. In a way that was exactly what he would attempt to do now – produce something unbased on facts, but which would still make sense.

He put down his still full glass and said, 'Well, gentlemen, I don't need to tell you why we are here in Singapore and that we're waiting hourly for the Japs to make a move.'

But even in the light of that statement, his words caused a ripple of excitement among the assembled officers. It reminded them that sooner or later they *would* be going to war with a new enemy – Japan.

'So far,' the admiral continued, knowing he had their attention now, even that of his staff who knew the facts, but who also knew he would have to make the final decision, 'we have nothing concrete – nothing hard and fast to go on – save the old hand's feel,' he touched his nose, as if that explained his loss of a precise explanation, 'for a dicey situation. And the situation is dicey. The native population obviously know something, for instance. The Sikh police commissioner is reporting a growing number of men going sick or absent without leave; the Chinese *amahs* are asking their employers three times the going rate for wages, knowing that they won't get the increase, only the sack; the Indians and Tamils are beginning to stockpile rice, their stable foodstuff – that sort of thing. Something's going to happen – and happen soon.'

He paused and let his words sink in. From

outside came the mournful wail of a tug's siren as it crawled through the late afternoon mist, like that of some lost soul.

'Now what's our position in the middle of all this?' the little admiral continued.

No one answered. They all knew it was a rhetorical question. Besides, they knew, too, that 'Tom Thumb' was better informed on their present situation than even their own intelligence officers.

'I shall tell you. The Admiralty didn't want us sent out here to Singapore in the first place. They favoured Ceylon, where a large fleet could be gathered in time, including an aircraft carrier.' He emphasized the word as if it were important and those in the know nodded silently. Their little group had only their own observation aircraft together whatever support the RAF could give them, which was very little. 'But their Lordships were overruled by Mr Churchill,' the little admiral gave them a wry grin, 'and we all know just how persuasive *he* is.'

A few of them laughed drily, but not many. They all knew, if the admiral was addressing them in this manner, straight from the shoulder, that the situation was too serious for humour.

'So here we are. Two battlewagons and

139

four destroyers to deter the whole Jap Imperial Fleet. Naturally,' he shrugged carelessly, 'it's not on.'

Now there was a murmur of agreement from the senior officers present and Captain Tennant of the *Repulse* looked very stern.

'So, gentlemen, I have made some rough-and-ready contingency planning,' the little admiral continued. 'If the balloon goes up, Singapore harbour will be too hot to hold us. We'll be sitting ducks for the Jap dive-bombers. The answer to that particular problem is *not* to be here in that particular eventuality.'

Most of those present looked puzzled or blank, but those senior officers who were already guessing what 'Tom Thumb' had in mind looked relieved.

'There are two possibilities open to us, gentlemen, and both in my humble opinion are better than staying here cooped up in Singapore harbour waiting for the Japs to drop something unpleasant upon us from a great height.' His attempt at naval humour fell flat. His officers were too concerned, so the admiral ploughed on grimly, for-mulating his thoughts as he spoke them. 'My first plan is to send your ship, Captain Tennant – the *Repulse* – with a destroyer escort to Port Darwin in Australia. We'll put it out that you're on a training cruise to shake down all those H.O. men in your crew. In reality, you'll be checking on the feasibility of using Port Darwin as a base in case of war with the Japs.'

Tennant lifted the pipe he was smoking 'cold' out of his mouth and nodded his understanding. His broad, humorous face revealed nothing, but inside his brain was already racing as he worked out the details of what he would soon have to do.

'In the meantime,' the admiral continued, 'the rest of the force will sail too, heading into the South China Sea but in constant contact with Singapore HQ here in case they attempt to recall us.' He paused and let out a sigh like a sorely tried man who was being forced to bear an impossible burden. 'It's not the best of plans, I'd be the first to admit. But it does have the advantage that both forces will be at sea where we'll have the ability to manoeuvre if trouble starts. Here we're just sitting ducks.' He paused and one of his staff handed him the waiting glass of pink gin. He downed it in one as his officers watched him intently, as if for some reason or other it was vitally important to do so.

For a few minutes silence reigned in the hot wardroom, broken only by the steady sound of the Ministry of Works' clock on the wall, ticking away the seconds of their lives with metallic inexorability.

'When, sir?' Captain Leach of the *Prince of Wales* finally broke the brooding silence.

'I've decided, Captain,' the little admiral answered, 'that the *Repulse* and her escort will slip away from Singapore during the night of the third of December. I'm sure that she won't go unobserved,' he added a little wearily. 'The Japs have had spies here for years. They'll be watching her depart. But you'll observe absolute radio silence, Captain Tennant, although naturally you'll be able to receive my signals. At all events we'll give out the poop that you're on a training cruise – but with no destination.'

Tennant nodded, his face grim, all humour vanished from it now.

'At all events *that* will keep Jap Intelligence busy for a while trying to discover it.'

'And the *Wales*, sir?' Leach enquired softly.

'We shall sail, too, perhaps twenty-four hours earlier, just to make it more difficult for the Japs – I hope.' He shrugged again and clutched the empty tumbler tighter in his little hand. 'Not much of a plan, I suppose,' he added, almost as if he were speaking to himself. Then his face brightened and he said, forcing energy and enthusiasm into his voice, 'From this moment on, gentlemen, there will be only happy faces in this wardroom.' He gestured to his flag-lieutenant. 'More pink gin, Harry,' he commanded.

'Ay ay, sir,' the young officer responded, his face reflecting his touching faith in 'Tom Thumb's' ability to steer a clear course for his ships and their crews. 'Coming right up, sir,' He pressed the button for the mess stewards, while the little admiral turned his face away to hide the tears in his eyes ...

And below, Big Slack Arse put down his two-week-old copy of the *Daily Mirror*, and said apropos of nothing, 'I think Jane's tits have grown since I last saw the "*Mirror*".' *

'Oh ay,' Little Slack Arse answered without enthusiasm.

Further up the mess someone was singing tonelessly, '*And the mate at the wheel had a bloody good feel at the girl I left behind him ... where was the engine driver when the boiler bust ... they found his bollocks and the same to you.*'

*Jane – famous wartime cartoon character.

'Put a frigging sock in it, arse-with-ears!' Little Slack Arse stopped him when he was in full flow.

The young rating turned on him with, 'I was only singing, Stripey.'

'Oh that's what yer call it, eh. Well don't.' He dismissed the red-faced young sailor and turned back to his old 'oppo'. 'Well, what do you think?'

Big Slack Arse looked at him, 'Do I walk across the water ... am I Jesus frigging Christ?' he snapped with an irate look on his woebegotten, lined face. Then he shrugged. 'I don't know, old matey, but I think this time we're for the chop.'

'The chop!'

'Yer, you heard me. It stands to reason, don't it. We're up the creek without a paddle. You know, Japs and everything.'

Little Slack Arse looked thoughtful, sucking at his teeth as he did so. 'What's to do then?'

'Not much we can do, old mucker. Die young and make a pretty corpse,' he said quietly, as if it were simply a fact of life. He opened the battered, well-thumbed copy of the *Daily Mirror* once more and started studying 'Jane's tits' again, as if they were a matter of great importance.

Outside, Singapore settled down for the night. Those who could, slept. A few said their prayers, but not many...

Five

'THREE'

With one last desperate burst of energy, Major Nairs burst into the bungalow proper. An Imperial Guardsman raised his rifle but Nairs shot him on the hoof. The man's face smashed in a welter of broken bone and thick goo. It looked as if someone had thrown strawberry jam at it. He went down whimpering.

Nairs sprang over the dead body of the brave old bearer. Next to it, a young girl lay, dead or unconscious, blood trickling a dark red down the inner thighs of her spread legs. He saw Susi. Her face was puffed and bruised. She lay spreadeagled on the table, naked, save for one shoe. He thought she was unconscious. But even as he ran towards her through the debris-littered, shattered room, he knew he was wrong.

He was. She was dead. He gasped, shocked beyond measure at the great gory gap ripped in her lovely stomach. For an instant all the rage and the fight seeped out

146

of his big body. He let his arm droop, as if in defeat. The revolver almost fell from his abruptly nerveless fingers.

'*Sir!*' Nobby's urgent cry of warning brought him to his senses and he looked up. A sinister-looking Jap officer was advancing towards, swinging his curved sword from side to side, a look of sadistic triumph on his face. Nairs pressed his trigger. Click – and nothing. The weapon had jammed!

The Japanese officer registered the failure at once. 'You – die,' he hissed in English. Next moment he swung the Samurai sword and brought it down in a great silver rush of air. His face contorted with rage and cruelty he aimed directly at Nairs' bent head.

But Nairs was not fated to die – just yet.

At the door, swinging on its broken hinges at a crazy angle, Nobby loosed off a volley from his hip. At that range he should not have missed. But he did. Instead of hitting the Jap officer, his slugs slammed into the blade of the curved sword. There was a great bell-like ringing noise and Moto yelped with pain as an electric shock shot up his sword arm. He couldn't help himself. He had to let the scarred blade fall to the floor.

Nairs raised his revolver. Now his eyes burned with rage as he realized fully for the first time what these cruel, little men had done to his beloved Susi. Moto cowered in front of him. He raised his bleeding hand in front of his face, as if he would could ward off a bullet thus. But Colonel Moto was not fated to die – just yet.

In that same moment that Nairs took first pressure on his trigger, ready to blast the evil Asiatic off the face of this earth, there was the tremendous ear-splitting roar of a plane coming in very low. Outside, the palm fronds were lashed back and forth by the prop wash. The parched grass swayed and the clothes of the dead lying everywhere were pressed close to their skinny bodies as the great black shadow swept across the compound.

The sudden appearance of the French seaplane – for that was what it was – caught Major Nairs completely off guard. Nobby, too. He glanced upwards instinctively. A small white parachute, not much bigger than a man's standard handkerchief, was swaying down out of the burning sky as the seaplane winged its way upwards.

Colonel Moto didn't wait for a second invitation. As Nobby recovered almost and plugged a Sikh who was just about to bring his lead-tipped stave down on the Major's skull, Moto tensed. The man screamed horribly and fell at Nairs' feet. And in that same instant, Moto went diving through the shattered window frame to his right, showering the room with broken bamboo and torn canvas shades. Nairs fired. But it was already too late. Moto and his troops were retreating through the jungle, vanishing into the dense undergrowth within ten yards or so of the kampong, the only sign of their passing being the dead sprawled in the extravagant, grotesque postures of those violently done to death – and a live naked baby, sat in the middle of the ruined compound, bawling its head off.

'Sir ... sir ... *please*, sir!' Nobby had urged desperately, trying to shake Nairs from his reverie as he stared down at the dead tortured body of his wife, Susi, face blank, registering no emotion. 'I know it's hard, sir. But we've got to move on, sir ... while we've got time.'

It had taken what seemed an age before Nairs had finally started to come round. By then the good corporal that he had once been in the Old War with had armed the Tamils with the weapons he had taken from the dead, though he knew if the Japs appeared again they would throw away their newly acquired weapons and make a run for it for they were such timid, humble people; arranged a burial party to carry away the dead for the funeral pyre; and organized bearers and rations – he knew they had to get out of this endangered spot, which was too close to the coast for his liking, as soon as possible.

It was only then that he had been able to drape a curtain over Susi's naked, defiled body, nod to the waiting burial detail and lead Nairs into the other room where he prepared to show him what had fallen from the French seaplane.

It seemed to take Nobby an age to make Nairs understand the meaning of the note scribbled on a rough piece of paper. The Japanese characters, which were decidedly shaky from the movement of the plane in which they had been written, they couldn't understand anyway. But it was the sketch map drawn underneath which Nobby thought gave some meaning to the message, especially the two letters in Latin script adorning the objects sketched in the basin.

'It's Singapore all right, sir,' Nobby said several times before Nairs finally nodded his head to indicate that he understood. 'A couple of years ago when I took a leave there, I went up for a ten-bob spin in an old Sopwith – that was hairy, I can tell you. The bloody thing was held together with spit and chewing gum, I can tell you ... Anyway,' he stopped himself in time, knowing that the Japs would be back once they had collected themselves, and they had to be off soon, 'I got a good look at the place. Yes, I'm sure it's Singapore.'

'I see,' Nairs said thickly, as if he were finding it difficult to speak.

Nobby, only too aware of the urgency of the situation, would have dearly loved to have shaken him into real awakeness, but he knew that wasn't to be. His whole being was absorbed totally with the terrible death of his young wife. All the same he knew the urgency of the situation. Now he felt he knew what the Japs had been after all the time. 'Just take another gander at it – just one small butcher's,' he pleaded with the dazed officer. 'To please me, sir.'

Nairs made no response and Nobby stared a little helplessly at his officer's face, fine-honed and scarred where the killer dog had lashed out before he had slaughtered it, and blackened and bruised by the fighting within the bungalow. In all the years they had been together since they had been young, he had never seen the boss look like this: pathetic, harmed, all hope apparently vanished. He knew he had to do something – do something drastic. On impulse he lashed out with his open hand – *hard*. It caught the OC a stinging blow on the left side of his weary, blackened face. His head snapped back and there were sudden tears of pain in his faded, red-rimmed eyes, 'What ... what the devil...' he stuttered.

'Sorry, sir, but I was forced to do it... Time's running out and we've got to do something about–'

'Yes, I know,' Nairs interrupted. His voice lacked its old decisive energy, but there was a look of purpose in his eyes once more and Nobby knew that his blow had worked. 'Well, what do you make of it?' Nairs asked looking at the paper Nobby was holding in a hand that now shook a little.

Nobby hesitated. He wasn't used to Nairs asking him for an opinion.

'Well?' Nairs queried, trying to take his mind off what lay just behind them in the battle-scarred bungalow, with a dead Jap sprawled across the veranda, the flies already beginning to buzz excitedly in a blue, greedy cloud around the great gaping wound in his shoulder.

'You remember you told me a while back about those new battleships, the *King George V* class?' Nobby asked.

'Yes.'

'Well, look at this shape and the letter 'W' on it in the Naval Basin – here.' He pointed a dirty finger at the Straits of Johore.

When Nairs didn't respond, the little cockney corporal went on urgently, 'Well, one of that class, if I remember from watching her launch on the newsreels, was the *Wales – the Prince of Wales,'* he looked up appealingly at his officer.

This time the information worked. 'Of course, Nobby,' Nairs exclaimed, 'that's right. Our most modern ship which took part in the hunt for the *Bismarck* early this year. But–'

'You see, sir,' Nobby cut in, trying to help him focus his attention on the map, trying not to lose him once more to his private sorrow. 'That's what it's all about – or I think it is. Those treacherous Frogs flew over Singapore in a recce. Probably our ack-ack people down below gave them the benefit of the doubt seeing they were Frogs. And they did the dirty work for the Nips. They located the two ships – I don't know what the other one is, don't matter – and attempted to pass on the info to those frigging Japs just now.'

'But why?' Nairs responded. His reaction was slow but better than before. 'Why, Nobby?'

'I don't know exactly.' Nobby's brow furrowed in a deep frown. 'But I do know this. The sooner we get to Singapore and some kind of civilization and warn our people that there are Japs already in the jungle and it has something to do with the *Prince of Wales* and that other ship in Singapore, the better.' He breathed out after so much hurried talk and waited for Nairs to make a decision. But before he could do so, it was made for him.

The afternoon's cloying, insect-laden silence was broken suddenly by a thick throaty twang, followed by a muffled explosion of a kind both of them hadn't heard since 1918.

Next moment a dark object came whirling over the canopy of trees trailing white smoke behind it, to land in the middle of the kampong. Almost immediately bone-dry bamboo and piles of straw started to burn fiercely.

'The Japs,' Nobby gasped. 'They're using one of their knee mortars, potting us with incendiary shells.' He meant the little Japanese mortars that didn't need a baseplate but which could be fired by one soldier using his knee as a rest for the firing tube.

'What?' It seemed to take Nairs a long time to grasp the meaning of the smaller man's words.

Nobby didn't give him chance to ask a second time. Instead he thrust away the precious piece of paper dropped from the seaplane, grabbed Nairs by the hand and dragged him to his feet. 'Come on, let's scarper, sir.'

'But Susi–' Nairs started to protest. However, already that particular problem was being taken care of. Presumably the unseen Japanese mortarman thought they were still hiding in that house of death, for now he dropped two incendiaries neatly on the bungalow's roof. It caught fire immediately as the glowing, greedy white phosphor spread out in a shower of red-hot balls, catching the bone-dry fabric of the makeshift place on all sides.

'*Susi!*' the cry came straight from the heart, desperate, dramatic, final.

Nobby caught Nairs just in time. 'No good, you can't get in there,' he cried frantically above the crackling flames, as they spread greedily to engulf the whole bungalow and yet more bombs came tumbling out of the leaden, overcast sky to add to the conflagration. 'Sir ... IT'S NO GOOD ... LEAVE HER, SIR!' he shrieked with all his remaining strength.

Finally he got through. Nairs' shoulders fell like those of a man who had recognized at last that he had been beaten. Tamely, he allowed Nobby to take him by the hand and let himself be towed at a staggering, stumbling half-run towards the cover of the jungle. Moments later they had vanished into the deep foliage as if they had never been there in the first place.

Behind them they left the dreams of twenty years ablaze, burning away furiously, and Susi's beautiful body being steadily consumed by the flames; and Colonel Moto, whipping the backs of the reluctant Sikhs with the flat of his sword, crying 'Speedo ... Speedo, you pigs–,' knowing that for him, too, time was running out – fast...

Six

Now the Western World waited. Those in power and with the knowledge knew the Japanese would move soon. They *had* to. Their supplies of rubber, tin, and oil were running out fast. The American-imposed embargo on the sale of these products vital to a war economy such as the Japanese was crippling. In the Japanese capital, Tokyo, not a single taxi ran that first week of December 1941. Soon the Imperial Forces' tanks and warships wouldn't be able to run either.

Perhaps this was what that great, leonine-headed, crippled president in Washington's 1600 Pennsylvania Avenue wanted. He wanted to force the Japanese into the attack so that he could bring the United States of America into the war on the side of democracy at last. No one knew. The man-in-the-street remained in the dark as usual. They saw the Japanese emissaries come and go in their striped suits and silk hats. They heard the weighty pronouncements from the US State Department. But the diplomats, for all their smiles and gestures in front of the newsreel cameras, might well have been speaking a foreign language as far as they were concerned.

The Japanese, still pleading, cajoling and occasionally threatening in Washington, were beginning to lose heart. Their messages, decoded almost most as soon as they were dispatched from the American capital for the benefit of his Divine, Imperial Majesty in Tokyo, showed they were rapidly growing ever less sure of finding a solution to the problem of the embargo. The price the Americans were asking was too high. The 'Sammies', as they called the Americans behind their backs, wanted no less than that the Japanese Army should evacuate all of China that it had conquered over the last bitter decade and withdraw from French Indo-China; and that was something the army warlords refused to do. Even Emperor Hirohito could not make the generals do that. The loss of face would be too great. They would be forced to commit suicide.

From the icy wastes of northern Manchuria down to the steaming jungles of South Vietnam, the Japanese troops massed. Already the initial assault formations were at sea, the troop transports packed with the veterans of the long war in China, heading for Guam, wake Island, Malaya, the Dutch East Indies. With them went the great Imperial Fleet, observing strict radio silence with the scout planes probing the way ahead with orders to shoot down every and any plane they encountered. No one was going to reveal the great secret – that Imperial Japan was on the verge of an all-out attack!

It was to be all or nothing. Japan aimed at destroying three empires no less – those of Britain, Holland and America. If she failed, Japan, the Land of the Rising Sun, would be thrown back to those days before Commander Perry of the US Navy had first forced the opening of their backward country. If Japan succeeded, on the other hand, it would create a huge new empire, extending from Australia in the south to the Russian border in the north and from – and including – India to the other side of the Pacific Rim, perhaps even the vaunted United States of America itself! It would be an empire of a kind never before seen in the whole history of the human race, an empire created by 100 million peasants who still worshipped their emperor as a God on whom they never dare look – why, when he passed spectators were barred from upper-storey windows so that they couldn't look down upon this divine creature!

The planners had long given thought to how they would attack, even more now that their resources were limited and they had to capture other raw materials needed for their fleets and armies swiftly. For them the primary consideration was to destroy the fleets of Britain and America which were really the only effective links between those countries' far flung possessions. How were they do this? The Japanese planners thought the problem could be solved very simply. Combined sea, air and, possibly, land forces would attack the great US base of Pearl Harbor and the British one at Singapore.

The year before the Japanese had observed with interest how antiquated British biplanes – Gladiators, Swordfish and the like – had put an end to the Italian dictator Mussolini's declared ambition to turn the Mediterranean into an Italian *mare nostrum* by surprising the main Italian fleet at anchor at the southern Italian harbour of Taranto. The British had done something which had never been done before – indeed no one ever had thought it *could* be done. Air power had overcome sea power. That day, though most great powers had not realized it, the battleship had become as dead as a dodo. Japanese admirals *had*, however, recognized that amazing fact. What they hadn't realised was that the battleship had been replaced by the aircraft carrier. When they did, it would be too late for Japan. But as the Empire of the Rising Sun edged ever closer to an outright war by the hour, the Japanese believed – and with some truth, too – that if they destroyed British sea power at Singapore and American sea power at Pearl Harbor, they could pick up the rest of the Anglo-American empires just where and when they wanted to; for those two great sprawling empires would be without the overall protection of seaborne forces. They could capture the various pieces – islands, countries, peninsulas – one by one and in every case be in superior strength. It was a plan that made even that mild-mannered botanist Emperor Hirohito gasp with surprise when they first told him of it in the overheated confines of one of the Imperial green-houses...

Back in the third week of November 1941, the Japanese planners had dispatched the attack force to the remote, fog-bound northern islands of the country. There to the surprise of the citizens of Kagoshima, in the area's south, one morning 350 dive-bombers and bombers came racing in from six aircraft carriers far out at sea. For an hour, the massive force whirled and dived and zoomed at almost tree-top heights across the city, sending the children and womenfolk running, cowering for cover, and the dogs barking hysterically, while they practised their complicated manoeuvres.

Then, as abruptly as they had come, the bombers disappeared, leaving a loud echoing silence behind them that seemed to go on for ever and ever. The practice attack for the real one to come soon at Pearl Harbor had been successful!

Now the great fleet disappeared altogether for the remote, permanently fogbound anchorage of the Kurile Islands, there to wait for the call to arms. But unknown to the Japanese planners who thought they had accounted for every contingency, they were actually being watched. Thousands of miles away, in remote sites in the former Italian colonies in East Africa, Ceylon, an obscure Victorian mansion in the English home counties, a farmhouse outside Alexandria, dedicated men and women, some of them who had devoted all their whole lives to tasks of this nature, listened in to the coded Japanese radio traffic, spending hour after hour, day after day, week after week, trying to discover the future enemy's intentions.

In the last week of November the great Japanese fleet sailed south for the area, from whence they would launch their attacks. They sailed in total, absolute radio silence. That fact almost broke the hearts of those devoted crypto-analysts who had followed the Japanese progress so far. What were they going to do? Their political masters – Churchill and Roosevelt – were crying out desperately for news. The fate of the Western World seemed to balance on a knife's edge.

Then, when these pipe-smoking ex-dons, Jewish naval petty officers, blue-stockinged lady maths experts, were ready to despair, someone – today it is not known who – came up with a simple – a very simple – solution to their problem. If the Japs were going to attack, which it was obvious they were, they would need to know the weather, not only in their local area, wherever that might be, but throughout most of the Far East. But on board the headquarters ships they didn't have the facilities for that kind of an operation. So where would they get their forecasts from? The answer was from Radio Tokyo.

Tokyo would broadcast the weather for the whole of the Far East – Japan had military and business interests ranging from northern China right down to southern Indo-China and beyond to the Malayan Peninsula. The vanished fleet would gain its weather, therefore, from the daily Tokyo weather bulletin. But which weather would specifically relate to the assault ships?

Again the problem was solved by those obscure middle-aged men and women, military and civilian, who would carry their secrets with them, in most cases, to their dying day. The relevant pieces would be in the 'Kano', which the Western cipher experts had been breaking bit by bit ever since it had first appeared in the late twenties.

Kano, which had been found to be a kind of cipher shorthand that was even more difficult to decipher, was always preceded by the word 'Kano' in the message to indicate to the recipient that a new kind of code was being slipped into the overall message. Now, ever since the Japanese fleet had disappeared operators halfway around the world had been listening to the Tokyo weather bulletins waiting for that key word to be inserted.

Thus it was on the morning of 3 December 1941, a middle-aged US Navy petty officer, one of the few who could speak Japanese and read the Kano code, was listening wearily to the usual long-winded Japanese broadcasts, distorted by static and other broadcasts as they flashed thousands of miles from Tokyo to the far-off US listening station. Suddenly he was startled out of his post-dawn weariness, longing for a second cup of strong 'Java', which he hoped might keep him awake during the long, boring shift to come, by a burst of high-speed Japanese. He could not decipher the language there and then. But he knew they were in 'Kano'. Hastily he started to note the series of Japanese characters, starting with the key words, as he found out later, *'Higashi no kaze ame'* – East wind rain. They were hidden in the middle of a weather forecast approximately two hundred words long and the already greying US petty officer knew instinctively he'd struck gold.

He had!

By nine that same morning, his first rough intercepts were on their way to the US Department of the Navy and although the US Navy's chiefs hated the British Senior Service with a passion, an hour later the same Kano intercepts were on their way to Bletchley, the British Government's top secret decoding centre, from whence they would go to the Admiralty in Whitehall and, more importantly, to Mr Churchill himself.

That midday, indulging himself in a good cigar and a stiff whisky before he went over to the House and tried to explain away the latest British defeat in the desert – 'Oh, my God,' the great man had murmured, head in hands when he had heard the news, 'when will the British Tommy fight?' – Churchill read the intercept. To most uninformed people, it wouldn't have meant much. Only that the weather was improving in the Pacific and that visibility for aircraft was almost perfect. But Churchill knew immediately what the sparse details, taken down by that obscure petty officer 5,000 miles away, signified. He looked up at young Colville, his secretary, who itched to be away to a fighting front instead of being a stripe-panted Whitehall flunkey, as he was at this moment, and announced grandly, 'This is it. War with the British Empire, the Netherlands East Indies, the United States and...' Churchill breathed a sigh of relief and took a sip at his whisky, *'no war* with Russia.'

He paused and young Colville realized that the Great Man expected some comment. 'But we are sure, sir,' he asked in the oblique manner of Whitehall, 'that Japan will involve the United States, as well as ourselves and the Dutch?'

Churchill laughed at the approach. 'We are – thanks to the Almighty from whom all benefits do flow. The President has been waiting for this to happen for years now. He is desperate to get into the fight for democracy against the fascist dictatorships, as he is wont to call them. Now he can call his reluctant nation to arms, not to fight for the *decadent Europeans,'* again Churchill laughed, 'but for America's own interests.' He took another sip of his drink and frowned, but only momentarily. 'Of course,' he added happily at the thought that soon he would have that all-powerful ally, America, which he had been depending upon to bail Britain out ever since the War had started back in September 1939, 'Roosevelt thinks he'll be able to ride roughshod over the British Empire in the process of helping us to win the War. But, my dear chap, as our cockneys say, *He's got another think coming!*'

The young secretary's mind raced. He could see that the PM was well pleased with himself. Naturally, he told himself, so he should be. Indirectly he had saved Britain's bacon. Yet at the back of his mind, Colville was uneasy, plagued by conscience in the manner of young men who had been hardened by life and the constant wearing away of ideals, vaguely grasped but there all the same, by the harsh realities of existence in the mid-twentieth century.

He would have liked to have asked at that moment, with the first snow-flakes of English winter drifting down slowly outside the great window, whether the PM would warn those who were going to be attacked by the gathering storm. But he knew that that would be a foolish question, one that the Great Man would have laughed at cynically if he had not been a person sensitive to the idealism of public school-boys.

It was as if the Prime Minister could read his thoughts at that particular moment, for finishing his drink with a flourish, he said,

'We shall hurry to the House, my dear boy, and encourage those old hacks and duffers for another day. It will give me the greatest of pleasure in a week from now to see their faces when I tell them that the little yellow men have launched – er – a *surprise attack*,' he emphasized the words cynically, 'and that the Japanese perfidy is being returned by a declaration of war on the part of His Majesty's Government and our cousins beyond the sea. It will take them some time to realize it, because the Mother of Parliaments, if you will forgive the cliché, is not exactly filled with the cream of intellectual society, but in the end they will. WE HAVE BEEN SAVED!' he chortled happily and gave one final puff at his big Cuban cigar.

Colville murmured something and went to collect the papers the Prime Minister would need for the House. As he did so he thought of those unknowns who would now die in, say, Singapore and Pearl Harbor so that the treachery of the Japanese 'surprise' attack could be brought home to the average Briton and American. But he knew that there was no use mentioning the matter to Churchill. He and Roosevelt in Washington would call the deaths 'acceptable losses', necessary to create the maximum publicity they needed. He sighed and guessed it had always been thus and would be always. The dead would simply represent bodies, no more, no less...

Outside, the snow continued to fall, slow and sad, like a white blanket. In a way it seemed to the impressionable young man that it symbolized the end of something and the start of something new. But what? He didn't know. In the end he gave up, as if it was all too hard to understand...

Perhaps it was.

Book Three: End Game

One

Nairs tensed. He sniffed the air. Besides him, Nobby Clark did the same. For all the world they could have been two predatory animals seeking out their prey. In fact they were – on two legs.

For twenty-four hours now, ever since they had escaped the mortar barrage at Camp Five, they had been on the run. They knew that the Japanese invasion of the Malay peninsula was a reality. They hadn't landed troops in force on the beaches around Kota Bharu, where they were expected to attack the most outlying British base there, but they had infiltrated small bodies of troops everywhere else on the same stretch of coastline – and not always in uniform. In the last twenty-four hours of alarm after alarm, the two fugitives had encountered wandering groups of armed civilians everywhere – and they were all heading south towards Singapore. Even when the two men, hiding in a bamboo thicket or mangroves along the trail, couldn't hear them speaking, they knew they were Japanese all right. The marks of their two-toed rubber shoes in the dust and their heavily laden bicycles, hung with rice, spices and ammunition, gave them away: the spearhead of the Jap drive southwards.

Now as the two of them crouched, ragged and worn, sniffing the air for that rank, fishy smell of the Jap – their bodies seemed to have absorbed the putrid fish sauce they used to spice their pre-cooked wet rice – they expected the worst: yet another enemy patrol barring their way and the delivery of that vital message to the authorities which might well mean the difference between victory and defeat in Malaya.

'Smoke,' Nobby hissed urgently. 'Three o'clock,' he added, using the soldier's way of indicating direction. 'Got it?'

'Got it,' Nairs replied, sniffing hard. But still he couldn't identify the smell which could only mean trouble. Instead he scented wood smoke and something vaguely familiar: a smell that he recognized, which all the same remained at the back of his mind, difficult to retrieve.

'Cor ferk a duck,' Nobby did it for him a moment later, 'Do you know what that is, sir?'

Nairs shook his head.

'Bully beef, sir ... bully beef fritters, sir,' the other man said excitedly, caution thrown to the wind now. 'Remember old Dirty Dick, the cook, the one that got his noddle blown off at La Boisselle–'

'Yes, I remember. Those breakfasts with rum and char and cowboy beans and corned beef fritters–' Nairs broke off the litany of the old war and snapped, 'They must be our blokes.' He rose to his feet eagerly, realizing for the first time the nervous strain he and presumably Nobby had been under ever since they had been cut off from their own folk. 'Come on.'

Eagerly, blundering out of the jungle, not caring that they probably sounded like a pair of crazed elephants, they dropped to the trail and at a half trot, they headed towards that delicious smell. They didn't get far though. They were stopped even before they reached the bend in the trail by drunken singing.

It was a drunken song they both remembered well from that same war in which a couple of slices of fried tinned beef washed down with half a mug of black General Service rum had been such a treat. *'M'selle from Armentieres ... M'selle from Armentieres ... never been fucked for twenty years ... inky-pinky, parlez-vous...'*

'What in the name of Christ–' Nobby began aghast, but the words died on his lips, as the bedraggled apparition came staggering around the corner into view.

He was an Australian all right. There was no mistaking that. A typical loose-limbed Australian, though more ancient than they both remembered the type from the trenches, greying, toothless in part, with his long, dirty khaki shorts hanging around his spindly legs. In his one hand he held a water bottle which obviously did not hold water and in the other he had a greasy fritter of beef which every now and again he attempted to bite with his toothless gums.

'Hiya, diggers,' he chortled happily, swaying dangerously as he did so, 'Have a bit o' tucker and something to wet yer frigging tonsils, eh.' The thought seemed to remind him that it was time to wet his own 'frigging tonsils' again. He raised the bottle and suddenly they could smell the heavy odour of rum as he poured a hefty swig down his skinny throat, his Adam's apple working all out as he did so. He finished, wiped his mouth with the back of a dirty hand and said, as if seeing them correctly for the first time, 'Poms, eh? What you blokes doing in this neck o' the wood, eh. Thought you was all back in Singapore, gorging yersens on tea and crumpet.' He laughed uproariously at the word 'crumpet', as if it was the funniest word in the English language.

'What's going on here?' Nairs asked severely, but he didn't complete the rest of his sentence.

Another khaki-clad figure, with the typical slouch hat on his shaven skull, had appeared round the bend. But this one wasn't drinking or singing; he was obviously *dying!* He staggered and slumped against the nearest tree, his nose pinched and very white, a sure sign Nairs had always thought of a man on the verge of sudden death. Down the side of his torn khaki shirt there was a scarlet patch which was spreading rapidly.

Without orders Nobby darted forward and caught the man before he fell. Carefully he lowered the dying Australian to the ground, saying soothingly, 'It's all right, I've got yer, mate ... it's all right.'

'Thanks, cobber,' the Australian soldier said weakly, his skinny chest heaving in and out in short shallow gasps. He lay there, blinking in the hot sun and Nobby attempted to pull down his slouch hat to keep the rays out of his eyes. But the Australian pushed aside his hand weakly. 'It's all right, cobber... Let me have a last look at her... Ain't she a beaut–' The words died on his lips as his head lolled to one side and even before Nobby had time to check his pulse, he knew instinctively that the man was dead.

The two of them turned to the drunken Australian private standing in the middle of the jungle trail staring at his dead comrade, as if he couldn't comprehend what had happened to the man; was he sleeping perhaps?

Nairs had no patience with the man; the situation was too urgent, especially with what they knew now of the Japanese intentions. 'What's going on?' he snapped. 'Where's your officer or NCO in charge?'

The Australian looked at him with that same cheeky look that all Australians – even those born in Britain – seemed to assume

176

when faced with 'la-di-da Pommy officers and gents'. 'Fucked off, the both of 'em, if they was lucky,' he said, his speech badly slurred now, 'croaked it if they wasn't. Anyway, as long as a bloke's got his grog,' he raised the waterbottle to his lips at the mention of drink.

Nairs was quicker off the mark. With one savage backward swing of his big hand, he knocked the bottle out of the drunk's dirty paws and barked, 'Enough of that now.' Next to him Nobby Clarke clicked back the bolt of his rifle significantly, as if he were prepared to use it immediately if the officer ordered him to do so.

'Have a heart, mate,' the Australian croaked, realizing that he was in the presence of sudden death, and sobering up considerably at the thought. 'Bloke's got to have a little bit o' what he fancies now and agen–'

'What happened, man?'

'Abo, a bunch of bleeding brown-arsed abos,' he answered.

'*Abos*?,' Nairs demanded. He knew the Australian drunk, who had the look of an outback redneck about him, would hate the Australian Aborigine with a passion. Still, for the life of him, he couldn't see how his

'Abos' had got this far from home.

'Yer,' the drunk replied, looking sorrow-fully at the rest of his grog disappearing rapidly into the undergrowth. 'Little brown bastards. Me and Blue just thought we'd have a little walkabout – nice bit of bully and a jar of grog or two – when the treacherous swine ambushed us.' He looked aghast. 'Just when we was gonna get our teeth into the tucker an' all. I mean what can yer say to that?'

'When?' Nairs snapped, eyeing the trail with suspicious looks now. He could guess what had happened. Just when he had thought they had out-run the Japs, they'd approached the nearest native village and suborned the local headman with threats, promises of rewards or both to turn on any lone white *Tuans* they might find wandering around the jungle. The two Aussies had been unlucky enough to have been taken for the hated 'Pom' bosses.

Nobby seemed to be able to read his mind again, for he said, 'Do we do a bunk, sir? And what about his nibs here, sir?' He jerked a careless thumb at the bewildered Australian. 'Do we take the drunken bugger with us or not–'

He never completed the sentence.

Suddenly the Australian's worn, craggy face was animated by a look of intense surprise. 'Strewth,' he gasped. 'What–' he belched as if he were going to be sick and Nobby jumped hastily to one side as a great gob of dark-red blood erupted from his abruptly gaping mouth, splattering everything in front of it a fearful red. The Australian staggered a few paces, hand feverishly trying to find the object that was killing him, but failing to do so. With startling suddenness he dropped to his skinny knees, still trying to pull whatever it was out of his back. Then they saw it – a primitive homemade spear of the kind they had seen the natives use when they had been out hunting wild pig, which were common in this part of the world. Now they had caught a two-legged one and it was dying just as noisily and with as much mess as the four-legged variety.

With the intense shock of the sudden pain, the dying Australian had evacuated his bowels. Red-stained turds were creeping out from beneath his baggy shorts and he was making choked, obscene noises as he fought Death and failed, crying pitifully in moments of lucidity. *'Don't let a mate down, cobber ... don't let a mate down–.'*

In the same instant that he dropped dead on his face, the faeces still protruding in slow obscenity from his stained shorts, makeshift spears rained down upon the two shocked, immobile observers.

Nobby reacted first. He loosed off a few quick rounds from the hip, counting them off as he did so. He knew the two of them were running out of ammo. Green leaves and broken bamboo shoots came tumbling down. A shrill shriek and one of their attackers, who had been high in a tree above the trail, crashed to the ground like a sack of wet cement. He bounced once and lay still, probably every bone in his body broken by the fall.

But as they started to back off, with Nairs having the foresight to pluck the big Australian's clumsy .38 revolver from its holster, together with the spare magazine pouch at his belt, the native attack continued. They came in on both sides of the trail. All the time they were trying to dodge the spears, they could catch glimpses of their angry strained brown faces, the bared teeth bright-red with betel juice. For the normally peace-loving Malays, they were too aggressive, almost fanatically so, as if they might well be drunk or drugged, or both.

Not that that mattered to Nairs. Their motives didn't interest him at that moment. All he wanted was to get the pair of them out of the ambush before the Malays got lucky and one of them went down with a spear stuck in to him, a spear which more than likely had been dipped in poison, as the Malays did when they went hunting pig. The poison paralyzed the animal and made him an easy killing.

Trying to keep as cool a head as possible, though both of them were lathered in sweat, they snapped off well-aimed shots left and right of the trail, trying to keep their attackers at bay; and they were succeeding. They knew that because they could hear the yelps of pain and anguished shouts as their bullets struck home. All the same, Nairs knew that soon they would have a problem – it would come when they tried to break off the action. Once they ceased firing for a few moments and started to run for it the Malays would burst forward out of the trees in full hue and cry; and although they had longer legs than the Malays, the latter were fresh and used to swift bursts of violent exercise when they were in the final stages of a hunt.

Abruptly one of the attackers, a big man

for a Malay, clad only in a sarong, his upper body muscular and gleaming with coconut oil, tensed as he raised a curved ancient blade, broke from the undergrowth. Ignoring their fire he came charging straight down the centre of the trail. 'Brave sod!' Nobby commented as he raised his rifle, prepared to let him have it through his brown guts. He reasoned as he told himself, 'That'll put an end to his frigging box of tricks.'

But that wasn't to be. Perhaps the Malay had been prepared to sacrifice himself knowing that the villagers had prepared this trap for any intruders, rushing them so that they would panic and not realize what kind of reception was waiting for them. They never did find out the truth of the matter. For in the moment that the tall Malay flung up his hands in mid-stride, they found themselves falling. The ground had given way abruptly beneath them and they were going down into the evil-smelling darkness, helpless and trapped, knowing that life had betrayed them once again before they could even realize how...

Two

Colonel Moto nodded his approval as the fawning Malay headman, puffing happily at the cheroot the Japanese officer had just given him, led him into the village indicating the two looted and burnt out Chinese shops and the fat merchant staked out in front of the bigger of the two.

He lay next to his dead wife, who was already bloated with gas and with fat dirty-white maggots crawling about the wounds the Malays had inflicted upon her, obviously to make her talk. They had failed and she had died too quickly. But they were taking their time with her husband, who must have been three times the age of the dead woman.

They had splayed him out on a piece of flat ground. Beneath him there were several young bamboo shoots, while his hands and feet were firmly tied to stakes driven hard into the earth, as if he were some yellow Christ being crucified in the wrong manner. He was presently unconscious. But he'd wake soon enough. The young bamboo shoots which the villagers had obviously watered several times were growing fast and Moto knew enough of the old traditional torture to realize that they would be neither diverted nor stopped by the living flesh of the human body, however strong that body was.

'The brown monkeys,' his interpreter whispered, standing close to Moto's ear, but trying at the same time not to breathe on his master for he knew the Japanese colonel's hot, unpredictable temper, 'are trying to squeeze the place where he has hidden his gold; the Chinks always have gold hidden somewhere. Look,' he indicated a group of Malay villagers beating a Chinese girl with the flats of their parangs. 'They think she might know, too. But the Chinks never tell their women anything.'

For a moment or two Colonel Moto rested his gaze on the tortured Chinese girl. Her face was already swollen and blue from previous beatings, but there was no denying her prettiness – she certainly was a cut above these women of the brown monkeys, Moto told himself, licking suddenly dry lips. He caught a glimpse of a small delicate breast, tipped a faint pink, that had penetrated through a tear in her smock, and felt his pulse rate quicken. Then, for the moment, he dismissed her. 'They have the round eyes?' he demanded of his interpreter, a curious mixture of Javanese, Ainu and Dutch.

'Yes, Colonel,' the interpreter answered in perfect Japanese. 'To be sure. This way.' Like some head waiter in a European restaurant that Moto had frequented during his time as a military attache on that continent, he stretched out his hand.

Moto frowned. He had caught a whiff of the man's odour. It was typical. He was definitely one of the hairy Ainu.* He could tell that smell anywhere. 'I shall wait to see them,' he decided. 'I feel in need of drink, food and pleasure first.' He gave an evil, self-satisfied smile at the word, revealing those gold teeth of which he was so proud.

Inwardly, the interpreter sighed. He knew what Moto meant by pleasure. 'Any in particular, Colonel?'

Moto pointed to the weeping Chinese girl.

*Ainu were the original inhabitants of Japan. Taller and much hairier than the average Japanese, they are looked down upon in that country. There is little inter-marriage between the two groups.

'That one. I couldn't stand one of those brown monkeys. Clean her up first and bring her to me. Tell my servant to get me out a bottle of sake.' His smile broadened. His role in the coming invasion was about done, he told himself. He had caught the two white men who could have caused problems. Now he could rest until the glorious troops of his Imperial Majesty placed the holy Rising Sun banner over Singapore and the British were defeated. Then he would take up his official role in the captured city-fortress. 'Go,' he commanded.

The interpreter bowed low and hurried to the group of villagers armed with the bloodstained parangs surrounding the half-naked, weeping Chinese girl. Behind Moto the Imperial Guardsmen and the Sikhs waited impatiently in the cloying afternoon heat for him to dismiss them.

Inside the hut on stilts, to which the jubilant Malays had brought them after they had been trapped in the pit used to capture animals which were a danger to the villagers and their pathetic pigs and chickens, Nobby hobbled with his still bound arms and legs from the slit in the straw matting and reported to Nairs. The latter's back hurt like hell – he had only just avoided the sharpened stake at the bottom of the pit, which might well have been tipped with deadly poison as they sometimes were, by landing heavily on his spine. Now he rubbed painfully at the bonds tying his hands together, the sweat standing out on his forehead like opaque pearls. 'Well?' he asked through gritted teeth, but not ceasing his attempts to break the straw rope by rubbing it against the shard of the water jug they had broken.

'Nips,' Nobby answered laconically, eyeing the last of the precious water dribbling away from the jug they had just broken. 'The same ones as before. Big long streaks of piss.'

'Imperial Guardsmen,' Nairs said, his breath coming in short sharp gasps, as if it was taking a lot out of him, this business of trying to break their bonds.

'For us?'

Nairs nodded.

Nobby sat down awkwardly, almost falling over as he tried to balance himself delicately on his bruised bottom. 'What's the drill, sir?' he asked, wishing at the same time that he did not need to ask the question. He knew that since his wife's death, his boss had little will to live. Neither of them had, in reality. They had both come out of a wrecked, depressed England for the job and to forget the horrors of the trenches, which had seemed to haunt them both relentlessly. Things had changed in Blighty since then. But there was no way back for them. They were too old, too set in their ways, spoiled by cheap living, cheap drink – and too much of it – and cheap women, half their age, who in other circumstances wouldn't have given the two rundown, middle-aged white men a second glance. They were yesterday's men; there was no place for them back in Britain, even in wartime. As he pondered their situation, he knew that they were fated to die here in a kind of self-imposed exile. All the same, that old rage that seemed to be built into small men – perhaps it was some sort of compensation for the lack of stature – burned within his frail, emaciated body. It was directed against the Nip pig, with his overlong 'toothpick', who thought now that he had the whole world by the balls; that he simply could not fail; that he was going to stick one up the old Empire's jumper and get a-frigging-way with it.

Suddenly he was fused by a new energy, a

kind of nervous trembling, as if he had been given a shot of 'get up and at 'em, lads' which had produced the adrenalin of the old days in the trenches, when the whistles had shrilled, the guns had stopped and old 'Snotty Nose' Smith 192 had growled, 'All right, me lucky lads, let's be having yer. *Up and over!*' and they had gone over the parapet, stumbling and slipping in that cratered lunar landscape beyond, whooping like a bloody load of drunk Red Indians until the Jerry machine-guns had startled rattling.

He flashed a look at the rattan mat which covered the entrance to the hut on stilts and then to a red-faced, sweating Nairs. 'How's it going, sir?' he hissed, noting the fresh blood on his wrists for the first time.

'Getting there,' the other man gasped. 'Give me five more minutes and then I'll ask you to give a tug at the rope. I think we'll pull it off then.'

'You'll do it, sir,' he attempted to encourage the officer.

'Course I'll fucking do it,' Nairs snorted. 'If it's last thing in the world, I'll choke the fucking life out of that Jap...'

The Chinese girl was terrified of him.

Colonel Moto could see that. She stood there, after the interpreter had guided her through the door and left immediately – the Ainu knew it was always safer to carry out the officer's command and get out of the way *quickly* – trying to hide her naked little breasts, fear filling her dark eyes.

That fact didn't worry Moto as he toyed with his sake. In fact, he was often pleased when women he was going to sleep with were afraid of him. It saved a lot of time. He had no time for the silly, white-painted geishas, with all that silly talk, tea ceremonies and fan fluttering. He was the son of peasants and peasant men liked their women quick and uncomplicated – and often. He indicated that the Chinese girl should sit down.

She did so and winced. He guessed that they had flayed her rump with their parang blades. That sort of thing gave the brown monkeys pleasure, simpletons that they were. It was not surprising that the millions of them had been subdued by a handful of round eyes and impoverished by a bunch of yellow Chinese coolies. They were such fools. Now they were exacting their revenge, only because they knew they had Japanese protection.

He indicated the stone tumbler on the mat next to the one upon which she was seated awkwardly, still clutching her tattered blouse to her girlish breasts. It was filled with sake. 'It will help,' he said in Japanese, not caring whether she drank it or not. He had no time for subtleties now. He wanted swift, uncomplicated fuck. Then he'd deal with the two round eyes and set off for Singapore, keeping out of the way of the flighting soon to come. With luck, he might end the war a general, when he would return to his native village to live off his pension and tell tall tales to patriotic young men, eager for some desperate glory.

She shook her head, as if she understood the Japanese.

Moto shrugged carelessly. He belched pleasurably. The Malays were Muslims. All the same they knew how to cook pork. The rice, pork and bamboo shoots they had just brought him had been very pleasant after the army rations they had been living off ever since they had left Saigon on their secret mission. Feeling replete, he opened the buckle of his precious sword-belt that dated back to some remote ancestor before a local Shogun had impoverished the family and reduced them to the level of the peasantry. He patted the sword as if to reassure himself that it was not too far away.

All the while she watched his every move through lowered eyes. At that moment, she seemed almost Japanese in the manner she kept her gaze dipped, as the civilians back home did to keep an observer from knowing what was going through their minds. He chuckled to himself a little drunkenly, as he wondered if she knew what was occupying *his* thoughts at that exact moment. For the Chinese girl had not noted that her artificial silk trousers had ripped at the seam between her legs. It looked very intriguing and he guessed that a Chinese merchant's daughter would be a virgin like the daughter of a similar Japanese merchant's would. After all, virginity in a bride-to-be always meant a large dowry, even among peasants who were not overly concerned with matters of morality as a rule.

He took another sip of the powerful rice wine and felt himself begin to harden. That pleased Moto. These days, as he confessed to his cronies back in Tokyo after a night-long drinking session preparing for the brothels to come, 'It's slower but more thorough... One day when I retire they'll call me the ... *the chimney sweep!*' That always caused a great burst of drunken laughter. Now, however, he was experiencing that old delightful tumescence more quickly than normal. God be praised, he told himself. I am not an old man after all.

The girl wriggled painfully on her sore buttocks once again. He swallowed the rest of his sake in one gulp. Why waste any more time? If he drank much more he would be incapable. Besides he had to finish off the round-eye prisoners before nightfall and be on his way. After all, the comrades of the two drunken and now dead Australian deserters might well be looking for them by now. He curled a finger in the girl's direction and patted his lap.

She shuddered, desperately trying to keep her breasts covered.

He laughed at her stupidity, but all the same, he wouldn't be brutal with her. Perhaps afterwards, if she performed to his satisfaction, he might let her live. The brown monkeys would soon punish her, once they got their greedy brown paws on her beautiful yellow body. But that would be afterwards.

He still continued to laugh when she did not move. Once again he patted his bulging lap like some patient parent waiting for a reluctant child to come.

But she'd seen the bulge. She shuddered and raised her skinny shoulders protectively, as if she half expected him to strike her. But his eyes were elsewhere than her shoulders. He felt some stupid boy again, who had saved his extra yen for months to enjoy the favours of some cheap whore for the first time. He was so excited that he could hardly control his hectic breathing.

He could wait no longer. Suddenly, startlingly, he lost his temper in that crazy Japanese manner that bordered on temporary madness. He tugged her towards him – but the next moment it happened...

Three

The big Humber staff car – *uncamouflaged*, naturally, the little admiral told himself – nudged its way down the dead straight road to the Singapore naval base, the red-faced Marine driver in his dress whites honking his horn furiously at the people and vehicles blocking the road everywhere. It was packed with Europeans and Chinese entering the place from the peninsula, via the Causeway, and Malays and the like leaving for Malaya by the same route.

Naturally there were the same prosperous pleasureseekers, European planters and merchants, fat Chinese, heavy with gold and flashy rings, even a few Indians, though mostly they preferred to stick to their own communities, with their guarded villas and compounds.

Yet again the little admiral was astonished by their serene confidence. They seemed to believe the confident government propaganda that Singapore was impregnable in case of war. Little did they know there were no plans for a mass evacuation of European refugees by boat and no air-raid shelters and defence infrastructure for those who wished to stay behind and flight ... and the admiral told himself, as he watched them, that one day soon fight they must.

Back at HQ, which they had just left, worried intelligence officers had told them that confusion was already widespread up in the peninsula. There were only two white battalions up there at present and some very young and relatively raw Indian Army units. They'd be no match for the Japanese veterans of the long campaign in China. Unknown planes were already beginning to drop crude leaflets over the native compounds in Tamil, Chinese and Malay, warning: *'Evacuate your towns before they are bombed.'*

'The meaning is quite clear,' the Intelligence people had explained. 'The Nips – and of course they're dropping the bloody leaflets – well, the Nips want the locals to think that they're out to just hurt the Whites, not them. That's why you see the natives do a wholesale bunk. They're getting out from under while the going's good.'

Now, together with Leach and Tennant of the *Wales* and *Repulse*, the little admiral made his slow progress back to the naval base with his mind racing electrically. It had been going like that ever since he had spoken to the assembled officers in the *Wales* wardroom. He simply hadn't been able to switch off. He *had* to make the right bloody decision – that's what it was all about.

And what a decision it was. If he carried out the plan he had already outlined to the officers of Force Z *too* early, he might well run the risk of finding himself and his two vital capital ships at the wrong place at the wrong time. If he left it too late, it could be he'd be bottled up here in Singapore's Straits of Johore, subjected to Japanese air attack. Trapped in those narrow waters over there, with only a handful of antiquated RAF planes to defend his ships, they'd all be damned sitting ducks. But in a way, his hands were tied by Churchill.

That morning he had sent a secret signal to the PM via the Admiralty for a decision, but he was still waiting for an answer – and every minute counted. It was so unlike the old bulldog. Despite his great age, old 'Winnie' was normally quicker off the mark than a man half his age. But not now. He glanced at his watch. It was almost three in the afternoon, almost time for 'tiffin' and still no answer. 'Bugger!' he cursed.

Opposite him in the big Humber, Leach looked across at him sharply, sensing the little admiral's tension, but not really knowing the reason for it in full. 'Did an oath cross your lips, sir?' he asked, trying to make a joke of it.

'It bloody well did, John,' the admiral snorted. He was in no mood for jokes, but all the same he knew he should have replied in a joking manner. It didn't do to let subordinate officers see that their superiors were worried. Bad for morale.

Leach looked at Tennant and the two of them turned their attention to the crowded scene outside purposely, knowing that they didn't want to embarrass the admiral, whom they now could see was a very worried man. Thus they drove the rest of the way back to the two great ships in tense silence.

At the other side of the world, in America and in the British Home Counties, the listeners, puffing their pipes, grimacing, scratching their faces, and in general going through the antics of very nervous people who were engaged in something that was making them even more nervous, were already working on the most recent Kano messages.

Fortunately the message was short and didn't take too long to decipher. The question remained, however, *what did it mean?* It read: 'Climb Nittakayama 1208, repeat 1208.'

As always the decoders had experts on hand – their establishments were filled with professors acting as temporary majors and lieutenant-commanders, who were specialists in everything from Sanskrit to Saxon runic writing. Nittakayama was speedily identified as a Japanese mountain. But what was the significance of climbing a 13,000 foot peak in Formosa, especially for a naval force? The 'profs', as they were called behind their backs despite their military ranks, soon solved that one, too.

Nittakayama was the highest peak in the Japanese Empire. Climbing it was regarded among Japanese as a great feat. 'As if one of our chaps climbed Everest,' one of the pipe-puffing dons, who looked if he could hardly climb out of his bed in the morning, opined.

'So you mean this is a call to war?' one of the decoders asked the 'Prof'.

'Yes, typical Japanese bombast. They love

that sort of guff.'

It was all the decoders needed now. The figure was easy enough to work out. '1208' meant the Japanese would start the war on the eighth day of the twelfth month – the eighth of December in other words.

An hour later the Bletchley* decode was in the hands of no less a person than Churchill himself. He stared at it, while Brooke and Pound waited tensely for his decision. Outside the barrage balloons guarding the capital rode up and down like fat, tethered elephants. Somewhere far away to the east of London, an air-raid siren was sounding its dread warning. The three most powerful men in the British Empire ignored it.

'Sunday next,' he said tonelessly, surprising the other two with the suddenness of his dry announcement.

'What, Prime Minister?' Brooke ventured. The sirens were coming closer now. Outside the shabby passers-by were quickening their pace. They knew what was coming: another of those 'tip-and-run raids' in which the German bombers dropped their loads of sudden death indiscriminately and then

*Centre of the British decoding operation.

headed below radar height for the coast and France before the British fighters could be scrambled.

'The little yellow gentlemen will attack on Sunday next.' Churchill did a quick calculation. 'That will be in the American time zone. It'll be Saturday in ours.' He took his eyes off the top secret message marked 'Ultra', which in a few minutes would be whipped away to the vaults under an armed guard with orders to kill anyone trying to obtain it. 'That means we've got three and a half days left before the balloon goes up in the Far East.'

Pound shot Brooke a quizzical look. The Prime Minister's bulldog face revealed little, but the former was sure that Churchill was pleased with the news. If America entered the War now, Britain would be saved. The United States were woefully unprepared for what was to come. Only her navy was fairly up to scratch. But once that great power, Pound told himself, started to flex her industrial muscle, nothing in the world could stop her. Churchill, who was half American himself, knew that well enough.

'What shall we do, PM?' Brooke asked, his dour Ulster face revealing nothing, as usual.

Suddenly Churchill beamed at him, as if

abruptly he had thrown off the 'black dog', as he phrased his moods of depression, of the last few days. 'That, my dear Brookie,' he said with new enthusiasm in his wonderful sonorous voice, 'is a very good question indeed.'

The other officers waited. Outside people were beginning to run, even officers, as air-raid wardens started to ring their bells, crying urgently, 'Everybody in the shelters, *please*... Raid imminent... Everyone in the shelters!' To the east there was the throaty bark of the first anti-aircraft guns opening up as the low-level raiders started following the wriggle and curve of the Thames, heading for their targets in Central London. The three men in the big eighteenth-century room, which had grown shabby and a little grubby since the outbreak of war in what seemed now another age, remained silent. What was happening outside – the sudden violent death to come – didn't appear to interest them. They were too intent on the fat bald man, dressed in his black suit, with the usual flamboyant tie, standing next to the window with its criss-crossed glass panes.★

★To prevent the glass being shattered violently by a bomb.

Finally, in the same moment as the first Heinkel came in sight, skidding over the shattered roofs of the capital, its turret gunner spitting tracer in a lethal arc, Churchill spoke. He said clearly and carefully, as if he had considered his words thoroughly before he spoke them. 'What shall we do, Brookie? I shall tell you. *Nothing!*'

'*Nothing,* sir?'

'Exactly.'

Outside now, the Heinkel seemed to fill the whole grey December sky. It blotted out the light as it came hurtling at roof-height, whipping off the slates in a noisy clatter with its prop wash. Somewhere a slow machine-gun had taken up the challenge – perhaps some Home Guard post on one of the flat roofs of the area. Red tracer sped after the two-engined bomber like a swarm of angry red hornets, falling short as the Heinkel increased its speed in its furious attempt to get away while there was still a chance. Behind, it left a cluster of deadly black eggs winging their way to earth.

'But why?' Brooke shouted, suddenly red-faced, whether from shouting or anger neither of the other two knew which. Everything – Churchill's strange lack of response, the tip-and-run raid, the rocking, trembling buildings like backdrops on a stage caught in a sudden wind – all appeared to fit into this crazy, absurd world in which they found themselves that grey December day in the middle of a grey war.

'Because we want the Americans to suffer a great defeat, you fool,' Churchill roared back, his eyes wild with the sudden excitement of combat. It was almost as if he were a young Hussar subaltern again, back in the nineteenth century, charging at the fuzzy-wuzzies at the Battle of Omdurman.

'But–' Brooke opened his mouth, his face registering his absolute, total astonishment at the Prime Minister's statement. But he never managed to pose his question. The 250-pound German bomb landed a hundred yards away. It exploded in a great yellow ball of fire, surrounded by thick grey smoke. Red-hot, fist-sized shards of jagged metal hissed lethally through the air. A woman warden went down with a helpless groan, her legs sawn away at the knees. As she fell, Pound caught a glimpse of long pink knickers – the absurdity amidst the grim final realities of war. Then a great cloud of dust and choking acrid fumes swept through the cracked panes and there was no time for further explanations...

It seemed pretty much the same to the little admiral, as the big Humber staff car, driven by the sweating, angry Marine corporal swept round the corner at last and the Naval Base came into view. There they were – the pride of the China Station: the great new battleship, which no amount of grey wartime paint and camouflage could disguise that it was brand new, and perhaps half a mile away in the anchorage, the sleek lines of the escort ship, the battlecruiser *Repulse*. How good they looked, he told himself, tears of pride in his eyes; for the little admiral was always emotionally affected by the sight of the ships he commanded. After a lifetime in the Royal Navy, ever since he had become a thirteen-year-old cadet, he had always felt that way. How could he be otherwise?

But as the Humber started to slow down and sailors in whites sprang to attention and saluted the car, while grizzled petty officers commanding shore work details commanded, 'Eyes, right...' – even the Chinese laundrymen they employed on board came to attention and tried to ape the sailors in showing respect – he felt a sudden wave of apprehension sweeping over him to replace the emotionalism of a minute before.

God, the little admiral told himself in an awed inner voice, there are thousands of them, mostly H.O. men, who a few months before lived in a world limited to pubs, pictures and palais de danse; who had never been to sea before save for trips around the harbour on some bank holiday or other. Now *he* was responsible for all their lives. Yet at the same time he was in the dark about how he could fight his ships – and he was sure that he would have to do so soon – so that he wouldn't fritter them away to no purpose.

'Penny for them, sir?' John Leach asked as they approached the gangplank and the bosun's whistle shrilled out its high-pitched notes in the time-honoured fashion of the Royal Navy which still sent shivers of pleasure down the admiral's spine.

He forced a smile. 'God knows, John–' he saw the worried look on the *Wales's* captain's handsome face and added hastily to appease him, 'I'm just wondering if that damned cook of yours is going to serve up that – er – speciality of his tonight for dinner. Don't think I can stand much more of it. The way it is I think I'll take up permanent residence in the heads.'

Leach smiled, relieved. So the situation was not that bad after all. 'You mean that curried cod of his and toffee pudding afterwards, sir. Yes, it does weigh a little heavily on the old gut. I'll have a word with him.' So they passed, chatting away, as if they didn't have a care in the world.

Watching them go, Big Slack Arse, not a man given to extravagant praise of 'officers and gents' normally, took the soggy Woodbine out of his mouth, spat noisily into the water far below in the bay, and announced, 'Not a bad old cuss, Tom Thumb. If anyone's gonna get us out of this mess, it's his nibs.'

Little Slack Arse looked at his old oppo cynically. 'You going soft in the head, matey?' he asked scornfully. 'Crap, said the King and a thousand arseholes bent and took the strain, for in them fucking days, the word of the King was law.' But then his tone softened and he agreed with his old comrade, 'Ay, I reckon if anyone can do it ... it'll be him.' They both lapsed into silence and stared down at the dirty water swirling around the keel, full of used contraceptives, paper and the occasional bottle. They stared hard, as if they could see something down there far below, known only to them.

Four

The faint shrill of a whistle, followed a few moments later by the quite clear command, 'All right, A Company move in on the right now. Let's be havin' yer, mates,' roused Colonel Moto from his pleasurable reverie. At his knees the Chinese girl stirred, but he held her in place tightly, still enjoying the softness of her tear-stained face against his naked loins.

'Get that trigging LMG* set up, cobber,' the harsh voice commanded some way away, carried towards the native kampong by the breeze from the South China Sea. 'Yer plates o'meat won't hit the ground if you don't move it sharpish there.'

For a while Moto was confused. He could not seem to realize the import of the calls. Were they in Malay? Did they come from the brown monkeys? Almost immediately, he realised they didn't. The Malays were softspoken, as befitted a subject people as

*Light Machine-Gun.

they were. No, those commands came from the damned black devils of round eyes who had thrown their weight around in Asia for the last two centuries.

He sat up suddenly, releasing his grip on the Chinese girl's head. He reached for his sword belt hastily and tied the buckle, while the girl watched him through lowered eyes. If he noticed her at all, he probably thought she didn't want him to see the look of shame in her eyes. For she had been a virgin. He had deflowered her the second time. There had been blood everywhere. Colonel Moto would have been mistaken. Her eyes weren't moist with shame. Now they were hard, angry and resentful, full of hate and the desire for revenge on account of what the bow-legged, cruel Japanese swine had done to her. Intently, while he did up his flies, head cocked to one side, listening to the sounds outside the village all the time, she studied the samurai sword. After a few moments she came to the conclusion she wouldn't be able to get it out of his grasp. It was too big for her and he'd be too powerful. But she did notice the little dagger the Japanese pigs used for hari-kari tucked into the side of the ornate scabbard. That she could use. Slowly, very slowly, she reached out her hand, as if she was about to touch his crotch.

Again if he saw the movement, he would have misconstrued it. His primitive mind would have taken it to mean that she desired him. He had broken her willpower. Now, like all silly women, after all those stupid protests and pleas of theirs, she had begun to want it. In the end all women became insatiable, unable to get enough of a man's penis.

He forgot the Chinese 'girl', as he had called her in a moment of passion, and concentrated on the noises in the jungle. He wasn't afraid, but he was concerned. Perhaps this was the rest of those damned big stupid Australians who had been blundering around big-footed in the jungle the previous day. If they were, he didn't want to involve himself and his mixed force of Imperial Guardsmen and Sikh policemen with them. His guardsmen were too precious. He'd deal with the two round eyes in the hut opposite and slip away with his guardsmen, leaving the Sikhs to 'defend the rear'. He smiled thinly at the thought, but there was no answering warm light in his eyes. They remained as evil and as ruthless as ever.

He made his decision. Now he could hear the Australians blundering through the jungle coming ever closer. Why were they shouting orders like that during the attack? They were giving their position away; they might well have been on some pre-war parade ground. Fools!

So engrossed with his plans and preparations as he was, he didn't noticed the girl's slim fingers on the scabbard of his curved dagger until it was too late. *'Hey!'* he called, as he spotted them, grasping for the little hari-kari dagger, 'What are–'

The words died on his lips.

In the same instant she lunged forward, her battered face suffused with rage and determination. He looked down aghast. His hands reached out. He tried to stop the lethal lunge to his stomach. Too late! He shrieked like a woman, carried away by the almost unbearable ecstasy of sexual pleasure, as the razor-sharp point pierced his skin, progressed into his guts, the blood spurting out in a scarlet stream over the dainty yellow hand. *'No ... no...'* he yelled, frantic with fear.

But there was no stopping. Perhaps she knew the details of the age-old hari-kari ritual; perhaps it was a matter of instinct.

But she continued the final act, as if she had been intent on disembowelling him in the traditional fashion. She grunted savagely, the hand holding the tiny curved dagger awash with warm, steaming blood, and jerked the razor-sharp blade upwards.

Moto's eyes seemed to pop from their sockets with the sheer, unbearable pain. He had never known anything like it even when he had been grievously wounded back in Manchuria as a young infantry captain. He choked, fought for breath, his legs already beginning to tremble and waver, as he forced himself to look down at his ruined guts. Something like a grey steaming snake had begun slithering out of the gaping rip she had made. It was his intestines. He opened his mouth to protest. But no sound came. He didn't know it, but he was dead already.

It was thus that the big Australian captain of infantry, together with the two newly freed prisoners found her in a ghastly tableau of death, as if frozen thus for all eternity: the dead Japanese slumped in his chair, mouth dropped open stupidly; the girl's blood-caked hand still holding the knife which had almost disappeared in the tangle of coiled guts which had emerged from her victim's yellow belly.

For a moment they simply stood there, unable to act or move, thinking the half-naked Chinese girl was dead, too. But then she moaned softly like that of a woman who had been ground down by the burdens of life and had come to the end of her tether – and they knew she was still alive.

That moan woke them all to their danger. They sprang into action, knowing that time was not on their side. 'Shall we take the Sheila?' Captain 'Rusty' Lantham, the big Australian company commander asked, eyeing the girl's nearly naked form with a certain degree of unprofessional interest. He looked just like all his soldiers, who addressed him as 'Rusty', save that he wore three pips on the shoulders of his shabby khaki shirt.

'Yes,' Nairs snapped. He knew they couldn't leave her now. If the Japs didn't flinish her off, after they had had their pleasure with her, the Malays would. They hated the Chinese, merchants or not, passionately. They blamed them for their own lazy improvident wretchedness. 'Come on.' He bent down and picked her up. Next to them, Nobby nodded his agreement and said, 'I'll cover you, sir.'

'Piece o'cake,' Rusty said easily, ignoring the savage snap and crackle of the sporadic firefight outside. 'My diggers could see the buck-teethed buggers off with one hand tied behind their backs. But I can't have any more losses. I'm going to need every manjack o' them. The whole frigging countryside is up in arms.'

Grimly Nairs nodded, took one last look at the dead Jap slumped in a pool of his slowly congealing blood – and Nobby knew why. He was enjoying the revenge the Chinese girl had taken unwittingly for the loss of his own poor dead wife, Susi. 'After you, Claude,' Nobby tried to lighten the tension with the current remark from the BBC's *ITMA* show. He pushed Nairs and the girl forward and followed, Lee Enfield rifle held tensely at his hip.

The surviving Japs of the Imperial Guard spotted them immediately. They turned their attention from the Australians pinned down in the jungle that fringed the compound and started sniping the little group. Nobby didn't attempt to aim – he fired blindly from the hip. He swung round from side to side, face harsh and bitter, pumping shot after shot at the guardsmen

214

like some Hollywood movie hero in the final shoot-out of a Western epic. 'Run for it – *now*,' he bellowed over the racket, as the closest Japanese pitched head first and dead over a kind of barrow that the Malay villagers used for hauling their rice shoots and the like from their paddy fields. 'At the double.'

Rusty grinned slowly in that masterful Australian way, which meant: 'No bastard's gonna tread on yours truly's toes without getting his goolies shot off,' and bellowed apropos of nothing, 'Who's pissing in my pond now?' Then he, too, was charging forward at Nairs' side, whooping crazily, as if he were enjoying every minute of the life-and-death struggle, blazing away with his big .38.

Now the surviving Japs poured on their fire. Slugs turfed up little angry spurts of dust at their flying feet. Chickens scattered squawking at their approach. The pigs followed their panic-stricken flight. A wild monkey, shot out of a tree, lay whimpering in the dust, clutching its bloody red arm, for all the world like a shot human.

But they didn't notice. They were too intent in getting away.

Over in the Australian lines the diggers,

never respecters of officers, even when the latter were risking death, were shouting encouragingly, or so they thought, 'Come on, Rusty. Let's see them twinkle toes flash, digger!'

'Arseholes!' Rusty gasped through the hail of fire, his arms working like pistons. 'Unfeeling shower of shit.'

A Sikh loomed up on their left. From somewhere he had obtained a parang. He raised it high above his head, a look of triumph in his dark eyes just below the caste mark. Nobby didn't give him a chance to bring it down on Nairs' bare skull. In one and the same movement, Nobby brought up the cruelly brass-shod butt of his rifle. Brutally he smashed it into the giant's mouth. The impact could be heard above the battle. The Sikh's turban tumbled off and his long greased hair flew wildly in all directions as he reeled backwards, spitting out teeth as he did so.

'Ta, ta for now,' Nobby gasped, using Mrs Mop's customary parting greeting from *ITMA*, and stumbled on.

Then they were threading their way through the jungle, ignoring the big fronds and palm leaves lashing their sweat-lathered faces, gasping like ancient asthmatics, blundering, as if sightless, towards the cheering Aussies, with behind them the Japanese fire slackening, for in that green maze the Japanese knew they had little chance of hitting the fleeing men.

'Over here, cobbers... Come on, Rusty ... over here!' the delighted Australians called to the fugitives. A moment later their calls turned to ones of delight, accompanied by wolf whistles as the infantryman spotted the long stretch of naked thigh, as Nairs carried the girl, trying to keep her body out of the thorns of the tangled undergrowth. 'Y've brought us a Chink Sheila,' they called, 'Good on yer, Rusty... Yer a white man, mate, even if you are an officer and a gent.'

For the first time, the Chinese girl opened her eyes which she had kept tightly closed during her escape, and asked in a typical Chinese sing-song accent, but all the same in a recognizable English, 'Who Sheila, please?'

'What a to-do,' Nobby exclaimed with surprise. 'She speaks English almost like what you and me do.'

'Missi on school,' she said, but already Nairs could hear the whirr and clatter of an infantry Bren-gun carrier churning its way up the jungle track.

'Get her in there Nobby,' he interrupted. 'Toot sweet.'

He handed his load to the NCO. Despite the imminent danger, Nobby was delighted to feel her warm nubile body next to his. 'Heaven 'elp a sailor on a night like this,' he chortled apropos of nothing. Next minute he was running with his burden for the carrier, with the slugs pattering off its sides like heavy tropical rain on a tin roof.

Behind him, Nairs waited for Rusty to give the order to withdraw. Originally he had come to find out the whereabouts of his two missing soldiers. Instead of the two most notorious drunks in the company, he had found Japs – and plenty of them. Now he did not want to lose any more men and fell readily into Major Nairs' plan to break off the skirmish and withdraw while there was still time saying, 'There's trouble every-where, Major, and "Old Blue", my CO'll skin me alive if I don't get back to him before the real balloon goes up.'

It was a decision with which Nairs heartily concurred, though he didn't enlighten the tall, rangy Australian with his overlong baggy shorts that the 'balloon' had already well and truly gone up. He'd save that information for afterwards.

218

Now with the Bren-gun carrier providing covering fire from the tight metal box next to the driver, the Australians backed off. With the fanatical bravery of the Japanese soldier, the handful of Imperial Guardsmen came running out of the undergrowth time and time again, bayonets flashing in the sun, faces flushed an angry, sweaty red, as they yelled that lusty cry of victory – or sudden death – *BANZAI!*

'I'll fucking banzai yer,' was Rusty's comment, as he and his men broke up their attacks time and time again, until in the end even Emperor Hirohito's Imperial Guard had had enough and the survivors vanished into the bushes, leaving behind a khaki carpet of their dead and dying comrades.

One hour later the two Bren-gun carriers, followed by a half-dozen three-ton trucks packed with happy and slightly drunk Aussies – Nairs wondered yet again where they managed to get the spirits from – were rolling down the red laterite road heading south to the Causeway, which crossed the Straits onto Singapore Island. The drunks were already singing and there were occasional shouts at bemused natives who watched them passing of 'Stick the place up yer gonga, mate... We've had it... We're off

219

home back to good ole Aussie.' And Nairs, listening to the hiss of the rubber and their happy drunken shouts and catcalls, could almost believe that they were really going to make it back to 'good ole Aussie'.

Five

'They say yer average Nip is a good infantryman although he's as blind as a bat' Rusty was pontificating, and it seemed to Nairs that even the Australian company commander had somehow managed to get at the 'grog', as they called it, although he hadn't left the little fifteen-hundredweight more than a few moments ('Taking a slash, cobber'). 'But I reckon nobody can beat an average Aussie when he goes in with the bayonet and entrenching tool. The Kiwi's not bad, but they're careful. As for you, Poms–' he left the sentence unfinished. Instead he belched and muttered, 'Manners ... pigs have none.' It was then that Nairs decided that the company commander *was* drunk.

'Garn,' Nobby said scornfully, but kept his voice low. Opposite the Chinese girl, her nakedness partially covered now by a couple of empty rice sacks, slept gently, apparently recovered a little from her ordeal, and the little cockney didn't want to bring her back

221

to reality – just yet. 'Yer old Tommy Atkins can beat everybody else into a cocked hat when it comes to fighting.'

Nairs smiled a little to himself. Cynic Nobby Clark might well be, but old-fashioned English patriot he was too – one of the old school who believed your average Englishman was a match for x number of this nationality and y of that. He told himself that they didn't make them like Nobby any more.

'Poms,' Rusty snorted without rancour, however, and not one bit concerned that he, a captain, was being contradicted by a mere English corporal of some sort of local abo territorials. 'Look what you blokes did at Gallipoli back in 1915. Those officers of yourn with their la-di-da accents and fancy monocles did for us Anzacs...'

Nairs let them drone on. That war was history now. Even he, who had taken part in it as a youngster, had forgotten most of it. The concern was the present conflict and whether all of them survived – Pom and Aussie alike – if the right decisions were made now. If the Japs really got a fast hold in the Far East and the Pacific, assuming the Yanks finally made their minds up to come in, there'd be all hell to pay. The Japs would dig in their toes hard – he knew them. They might be fighting to turf the little yellow men out of each individual island they had captured for years, perhaps decades, to come. Then it would be a matter of who had the longest staying power and knowing Western politicians, always primarily concerned with winning the next election, it would be the West which would give up first.

He sighed and winced at the pain of his wounds. What did it matter, he asked, as the little convoy started to roll through a thick rubber plantation on both sides of the dead-straight road heading south? Susi was gone. His job, too. He knew he was too old to make a fresh start especially after what he suspected would be a long war to come. He looked grumpily at the line after line of rubber saplings whizzing by. There were no signs of the usual Tamil labourers. But he guessed they had returned to their compounds. It was getting dark and the humble imported Tamils were scared of the spirits, ghouls and tigers which they maintained roamed the countryside in profusion at night.

Up ahead, though, he could see through the open front of the fifteen-hundredweight truck, there was some sign of life. A pile of thick black smoke rose like a solid pillar into the still pre-dark air. But strain as he could, he could make out no sound to go with it. Perhaps some damned fool had carelessly dropped a match after lighting his cheroot and had started a fire which was just beginning to get under way? It happened all the time. The Tamils were a gentle, humble, obedient people. But they were damnably careless. They had to be warned time and time again. But then, Nairs told himself, it wasn't their property. It belonged to some far-off tuans in a mythical place called London, where the 'King-Emperor' lived with his red-coated soldiers and magnificent elephants. Why should these humble Tamils, who owned nothing save the clothes on their back, care?

In the cab the driver, cheap cigarette stuck out of the corner of his mouth, changed gear hurriedly and murmured something. Nairs looked up surprised. Why was he changing down and reducing speed? The plan had been to keep going all night and, by changing their drivers at four-hour intervals, to roll on till they reached the Causeway. Even the easy-going Australian company commander had realized the importance of reaching Singapore soon, after Nairs had told him as much as he needed to know of the mission.

Nairs reached across and shouted above the racket the driver made double-declutching, 'What's going on?'

'Some sort of frigging roadblock ahead, mate,' he answered with typical lack of respect for an officer. In the Australian Army, it seemed to a slightly bemused Nairs, everyone was a 'mate'. Probably they called the senior Australian officer, General Blarney, 'mate', too.

'Keep your eyes peeled,' he warned and turned to the others, cutting into Rusty's discourse on why 'yer average Aussie digger don't take any bull from nobody, mate,' with a curt 'Obstruction ahead, Rusty. Better get yer finger out.'

The big rangy Australian was all soldier immediately, something that Nairs liked. It was comforting to have a 'bloke' like the Aussie and his happy-go-lucky fighting mob on your side. 'Got it,' Rusty snapped, hauling out his big. 38. 'There's a Red light flashing some kind of warning. Hey, Mike,' he addressed the driver, 'keep her in gear and the engine running. Go for 'em like a bat out a hell if there's any trouble. Got it, mate?'

'Got it, skipper.'

Nobby looked at Nairs in the gloomy light and joked, 'Well, they do know another word than "mate", it seems.'

Nairs said nothing as the little truck slowed down ever more and he felt the sudden heat strike him a damp clammy blow across the face like a slap from a chubby, soft fist.

'Hold it there,' a harsh Scots voice cried, adding a moment later, 'One man out at the double. Advance and be recognized. *Jildy now.*' There was no mistaking the suspicious tone and language of the old sweat. These were regular British troops all right!

'I'll go,' Nairs volunteered, as the truck slowed to a halt, though the driver continued to gun the accelerator as if he were ready for a speedy take-off in an instant. He dropped over the tailboard and noted immediately the Bren-gunner crouched in the ditch to the left, light machine-gun trained on the little convoy which was beginning to slow down everywhere. Further in the shadow of the gum trees there were other soldiers lurking, given away only by the dull gleam of their bayoneted rifles. Nairs told himself it was a typical pre-war Regular Army roadblock.

Presumably the Army Command hadn't yet heard the typical Jap tactic the latter had used everywhere in China, of flanking all such positions on roads and cutting the road to the defenders' rear. That usually panicked vehicle-bound troops to pull out.

He stepped forward and the harsh Scots voice cried, 'Who goes there?'

'Friend,' Nairs answered, as always feeling rather foolish at the standard answer.

'Advance and be recognized.'

Nairs moved the last few paces to the makeshift barricade and held up his officer's identification card to the light of the sentry's torch.

The little Scot, face an angry red and covered with pitted acne marks, stared at the photo for what seemed to Nairs a long time before finally saying, 'Ay, it's you, sir.'

'Thank you for telling me,' Nairs said gently, but even as he spoke he realized that irony was wasted on the Scot. In his turn, the latter swung round and shouted to the men crouched in the drainage ditch further on, 'Officer here, sir. Shall I let him proceed?' He was obviously pleased with the long word, for he made a great fuss of it.

'Yes, McTavish, let him proceed, please.'

Next to Nobby and the Chinese girl who

was now awake and worried, Rusty breathed, 'Strewth, cobber – *please*. My boys'd skin me alive if I dared use a word like that to them. They'd think I'd gone all limp-wrist and violet-scented hair cream.' All the same, he turned to the rear where the rest of the convoy waited and whirled his right arm around three times, indicating that they should 'proceed'.

A couple of minutes later they were through the roadblock, parked in the cover of the plantation and talking in a whisper, as if the Japs were just behind the next bush, to the company commander of the Argylls who were holding this stretch of the road.

Captain Stewart of that Ilk, as was apparently his name and title, wasn't a happy man. 'As far as I know,' he explained in a perfect upper-class English accent, without the slightest trace of Scottish influence, though it was clear he was inordinately proud of his Scottish regiment and heritage, 'we are not at war. Yet,' he waved away the midges which were becoming a nuisance now the light was fading rapidly, 'the battalion's in trouble everywhere.'

'How do you mean?' Nairs asked quickly. Now in the distance he could hear the faint rattle of musketry and guessed this was what the Scottish captain was referring to.

'Well, old chap,' Stewart answered like a man who had been sorely tried, fighting to keep calm and control his temper, 'we've been petrol-bombed, had the tyres of the rear echelon lorries slashed, one man kidnapped, vanished into God knows where, and now...' he cocked his head in the direction of the firing, 'that sounds like our D Company taking a bit of stick.'

'From who, mate?' Rusty asked, taking an obvious delight in addressing the high-class Pom as 'mate', though he knew the answer already himself.

'God knows. The native wallahs ... Japs ... some of our Sikhs by the look of it.' He shrugged. 'The whole of bloody Malaya seems to be up in arms against us for some reason I can't fathom out.'

Outside in the cover of the trees, one of Rusty's Aussies, who had probably been at the 'grog' again, was warbling very off-key:

'M'father's a black market grocer
M'mother makes illegal gin
M'sister sells sin in the Underground,
K'rist, how the frigging money rolls in.'

Stewart of that Ilk moaned, 'Won't that man put a sock in it? The CO would have a blue fit if he heard the bugger giving our positions away like that. His feet wouldn't touch the ground.'

'Have a heart,' Rusty began, but he never finished his words. Suddenly, startlingly, a shot rang out. Angry scarlet flame stabbed the glowing tropical darkness. There was a yell of pain and an Aussie voice cried plaintively, 'Some bugger's gorn and shot my frigging finger off – my frigging fornicating finger as well.'

But at that particular moment no one in the little camp was particularly concerned with the unknown Aussie's love life. Instead there was a blaze of musketry, with bullets zipping and cutting the air lethally, until a sergeant-major cried with all the frightening power of his high office behind him, 'The next soldier what fires off a round'll have his name taken.'

That did it. The firing died away, finally leaving behind it a loud echoing silence that was somehow eerie in those dark sinister woods so that it seemed to the more sensitive of the Scottish soldiers that there were enemies, sinister, unknown enemies, lurking behind each tree, just waiting ...

waiting for what? That they didn't know.

In the end, Nairs broke the heavy silence with, 'Gentlemen, I have something to tell you. It is of great importance. I would like your help to carry out my task.' He shrugged. 'But if that is not possible, then I am afraid I shall have to go it alone—'

'Not without me, sir,' Nobby protested stoutly, voice full of indignation.

'Of course not,' Nairs appeased him hastily. 'Thank you. But to my mission...' Hastily he started to explain, while the others listened in silence. But there was an air of unease about them and Rusty, for all his Aussie bravado, kept peering into the shadows over his shoulder, as if he expected some monstrous Nip to appear at any moment.

Finally Nairs finished with, 'You see, gentlemen, if I've got it right – and I think I have – it is vital I get to Singapore by tomorrow. And the way things are out here in the peninsula, I need all the armed help I can get. What do you think?' he ended suddenly in abruptly lame helplessness, as if he knew right from the start they would refuse him.

They did. Fifteen minutes later the decision was made. Captain Stewart of that

Ilk said a little miserably, 'I've talked to the CO, Major and he says it's impossible without orders from Brigade. And he doubts strongly that the Brig would give orders of that nature.' He paused and added, 'I believe you, that there are really big issues at stake. But it's not for your ordinary common-or-garden infantry wallah to do much about such matters. You understand, don't you?' he cleared his throat, as if suddenly very embarrassed.

'I understand.'

'Yer, mate,' Rusty joined in. 'Like to oblige, but it ain't on. The CO'd think we're just a bolshy lot out after the grog and Sheilas. He's ordered me to stand fast here with the Scotties–'

The Argyll frowned at the word, but said nothing.

'Sorry,' Rusty ended lamely and looked at the toes of his big boots awkwardly, as if he were a little ashamed.

Nairs forced a grin. 'It's all right. Me and Corporal Clark here'll manage, won't we, Nobby?'

'Too right, sir,' Nobby Clark answered, with more enthusiasm than he really felt.

'Me, too,' the Chinese girl standing next to Nobby chirped, speaking for the first time in her delightful singsong English.

'You!'

Rusty touched Nairs' arm, as the latter turned to face the girl, as if to stop him saying more.

'Better off that way, cobber,' he said gently. 'If the balloon goes up here, well–' he didn't finish his sentence, but ended up with a hesitant, almost embarrassed, 'Well, we've all seen what the bloody Nips do to women, haven't we?'

'Agreed, sir,' Nobby added, 'if you don't mind me putting in my twopennyworth. Besides she does speak the Chink lingo and it seems to yours truly that the Chinks are about the only ones who are going to help us if we need help. The Tamils are scared of their own shadows, the Malays are out for number one and the Sikhs, well, they look as if they've gone over to the Japs lock, stock and barrel.'

Nairs gave in. 'All right then, she comes with us.'

'Thank you,' the girl said softly and Stewart of that Ilk said a little bitterly, 'Well, Major, if you don't mind my saying it, you'd better get on with it. This quiet won't last for ever.' He straightened up and saluted. Surprisingly enough Rusty did the same, saying. 'Best o' luck, Major.'

'Thanks,' Nairs said. He was not an emotional man by any means, but all the same, he was moved. He peered through the glowing gloom of the roadside, with everywhere the Jocks and the Aussies waiting for what would sooner or later come up that road, and felt he was seeing them all for the last time. They'd die at this nameless crossroads – he knew that with the intensity of a vision – fighting bravely for the far-off 'King-Emperor' to become a mere footnote in the history of the War.

Nairs returned the salute and then without another word turned and set off up the road that led south. Wordlessly the other two followed, with Nobby supporting the Chinese girl.

Behind them Captain Stewart of that Ilk broke the heavy silence with, 'Well, Captain, I suppose we'd better look at our dispositions, eh.' He was suddenly very weary, as if he had just realized that it was all purposeless...

Six

It was pitch-black now. Still they continued walking. They stuck to the road for the most part, but every time they came within sight – or really, smell – of a native kampong, they slipped into the bush. But they weren't very happy there, blundering through the tangle of undergrowth, alive with strange threatening sounds, which seemed even worse in the darkness. More than once they heard frightening slithering sounds and the Chinese girl clung even closer to Nobby, as if she suspected the sounds were being made by deadly snakes. Once, in a moment of relative silence, they were scared out of their wits by a sudden piercing, almost human, scream. Nobby felt the small hairs at the back of his neck stand erect with fear and the girl dug her fingertips into the soft flesh of his upper arm till it hurt.

Trying to calm the two of them, the old jungle-hand Nairs said drily, for the sudden shock had dried up his saliva, too, 'All right ... all right, it's only a bloody monkey.' But even as he said the words, he could guess just how taut the nerves were of the other two.

Dawn was never more welcome that December morning and now for the first time Nairs allowed them to relax and rest next to a clear little stream, with the water bubbling along its course sweetly. While the two of them scooped up the fresh water greedily, he moved off to check the tangled thick vine he had spotted some thirty-odd yards away. Drink was all right, but they needed food, too, and perhaps the vine, if he were right, would provide it.

It did. The large berries, looking for all the world like coarse, hairy chestnuts hanging from the vine, were rambutans, which provided juicy food. He pulled down a few of them, cracked them in the way he had seen the Malays do and crunched the nuts. They tasted good and surprisingly sweet like a mixture of fruit juices. He filled the pockets of his khaki shirt with them, taking them over to where the other two, replete and swollen with water, were slumped on the ground looking tired. He explained how to crack and eat the nuts, and while they did so, obviously enjoying the delights of the very sweet juice, he examined their shoes and feet.

By now even Nobby's army boots were beginning to suffer and the girl's shoes were falling apart. The best thing for her would be to walk barefoot, he told himself. But that, he knew, would bring problems, too. Used to heels, the pressure would then be on the shapely calves of her delightful legs. That would be very painful, he knew of old. So he compromised, tying strips of bamboo leaves under the soles, trying to keep them together with the tattered uppers. With a bit of luck they would last the rest of the way till they reached the Causeway. He yawned, finished, while the other two half slumbered in the growing heat of the new day and told himself that he could sleep for twenty-four hours solid once they had completed their mission. He had never felt as tired as this in his whole life. He was so exhausted that he was having difficulty in focusing his eyes and it was only with an effort of sheer willpower that he could raise himself and command, 'All right, the two of you, let's be on our way ... With luck we'll reach the Causeway by noon and then, I promise, you can sleep the clock round.'

'I'd give my left goolie to get some real shut-eye,' Nobby exclaimed and then, remembering the girl, added hastily. 'If you'll forgive my French, miss.'

The Chinese girl, dark circles of exhaustion beneath her eyes now, looked at him in bewilderment, but said nothing. Instead she rose stiffly to her feet and stood there in silence; Nobby did the same, though he made a performance of it, groaning loudly as if he were sorely plagued.

Nairs forced a smile. 'Come off it, Nobby, stop swinging the lead. Look at Irene,' which was the name they had given the girl at the American Mission School she had been attending before returning to the village. 'She puts you to shame, an old soldier like you.'

Nobby grumbled under his breath, but Nairs could see, exhausted as he was, he was happy in his own way.

'Good,' Nairs said, narrowing his eyes against the slanting, blood-red rays of the new sun piercing the tangle of jungle. 'Very quickly. It's my plan to get out of the thickness of this place and head back to the road. But we won't use it. We'll stick to the fringe of the vegetation bordering the road. That way we can do a quick bunk if we run into trouble.'

'Trouble, sir?' Nobby queried. 'Not this far south, sir, surely?'

Before Nairs could answer, the girl did for him. 'Trouble everywhere.' Like most Chinese speakers of English, she had trouble pronouncing the 'r's, making them sound like 'l's. But in her case, it didn't sound funny, more like an attractive girlish lisp.

Nairs nodded his approval of her statement and she said. 'No, we can't trust anyone. All bought Nippon gold.' She made the Chinese gesture of counting money with her thumb and forefinger in order to make her meaning quite clear.

And with that warning on the venality of men ringing in their ears, they moved – Nobby in the lead, armed with a hefty bamboo stave as well as his rifle, Irene in the middle and Nairs in the rear, also carrying a supplementary weapon. This time it wasn't a stave but a big army-issue handkerchief, packed with wet earth and tied up at both ends. To Nairs' way of thinking, it would provide an ideal black-jack if he wanted to knock someone out without making any noise.

Cheerful at the prospect of safety close at hand and refreshed from the water and the sweet, juicy berries, they set off at a good pace. To their left the laterite of the road leading south seemed empty. They had yet to see a vehicle, even one of the ox-drawn water or sewage carts which the natives used for irrigating and fertilizing their paddies. Once they glimpsed a group of Tamils on the other side of the road, bent among the trees, tapping rubber. But that was all. They might well have been the last human beings left alive on this hot December morning in the middle of the world conflict...

It was about ten that morning that they were alerted to the fact that they were *not* alone in the hot, sweltering world of verdant foliage, heavy with the odours of the jungle and plant decay, by a strange tinkling sound.

They stopped as one, the girl's heart beating frantically with alarm. In the fashion of women, her right hand flew to her mouth, perhaps to stifle the cry that might have otherwise issued from it.

'What d'yer make of it, sir?' Nobby whispered as the two of them crouched at the edge of the road, weapons at the ready in hands which were abruptly wet with hot sweat.

'Search me,' Nairs hissed and peered up the road, ready at a moment's notice to give the command to disappear into the jungle at the first sight of anything suspicious.

The tinkling sound grew louder. It sounded to Nairs like the bells used at Buddhist temples or those at mass in his long-forgotten Catholic youth. He bit his bottom lip. It didn't sound dangerous, yet one couldn't be too careful in this suddenly topsy-turvy world of Malaya in December 1941.

'Do we scarper, sir?' Nobby asked.

Nairs didn't answer, for with slow dragging steps, one hand with the stave extended like a blind man does when he searches out his way in unfamiliar territory, a strange, ragged, bearded figure had appeared. For a moment Nairs was reminded of some medieval woodcut by, say, Durer. Next to him, Irene tensed. She knew nothing about Durer but she recognized the old barefoot man making his way unerringly in their direction. She gasped something in Chinese, then added in almost awe-struck horror, *'Leper'*.

'Cor,' Nobby agreed. 'Yer right. Look at his hooter ... poor old sod ain't got one.'

Now that he had come closer with that strange rolling gait, Nairs could see his corporal was right. Where the old man's nose had once been there were two gaping black holes, from which grey noxious fluid drained, while the hand not holding the stave, wrapped in fluttering dirty bandages, was minus all its fingers. The stranger was indeed a refugee from some leper colony or other.

'What we gonna do with the poor old sod, sir?' Nobby began. But before he could carry on, the leper beat him to it. He tinkled the bells that were attached to the top of his stave and stared in their direction. He was giving them a warning, Nairs realized, that he was on his way – as a leper.

Transfixed, they waited, frozen to the spot, the Chinese girl's pretty young face contorted with fear as she sheltered behind Nobby, and the old man advanced upon them with that awesome, dust-dragging shuffle of his, which might have meant – Nairs thought – that the terrible wasting disease had eaten away his toes as well.

'Hold it – there,' Nairs said finally.

The leper shuffled to a stop. He turned his head slowly in the direction of the speaker, as if it was worked with rusty springs. 'An Englishman,' he exclaimed through bare gums. Despite that, his accent was perfect. He was an Englishman, too.

'Yes,' he caught the look of surprise on all their faces on hearing him speak the two men's language, though he was burnt as black as any Tamil by the tropical sun. 'A poor unfortunate compatriot, laid low by this terrible disease'. With an awkward wave of his other stump, he indicated the rotting flesh and grey encrusted weals on his bare shoulders and cheeks. 'Abandoned to his fate by an ungrateful nation.'

The vocabulary was as educated as the voice and Nairs heard himself stuttering, 'What exactly do you mean?'

'Mean?' There was an underlying bitterness in the manner which he repeated the word.

'I was like you once,' the old leper answered. 'I contracted this – er – disease and the Colonial Service abandoned me. There is no other word for it. There were no provisions for the ruling class,' His wizened old face contorted into a parody of the contempt he must have felt, for the leprosy was so far advanced that most of his facial muscles were paralyzed. 'So I remained here. But who should tend me? Who, you may ask–'

'I'm sorry,' Nairs cut in harshly, iron in his voice now, knowing that they had no time to waste on the bitter Englishman, stricken by this horrific disease. 'But we have things to do. Tell me, what is the road ahead like – the one you have just come down.' He hesitated, not wanting to appeal to the other man's sense of patriotism, for he guessed he would have none.

Surprisingly enough, he responded. 'I understand,' he said, lowering his head slightly as if he didn't want to offend them any longer with his wasted features. 'I have covered some two miles since dawn, trying to find some kind person who might give me a bowl of rice, perhaps even a little chicken. But I have seen no one, and the last village I passed through was abandoned. They had even taken their food with them, as if they had gone for good.'

He waited a few moments, as if he expected Nairs to say something and when the latter didn't, he said mildly, his former bitterness vanished from his reedy, old man's voice, 'Is that of some help to you, Major?'

'Yes ... thank you very much,' Nairs stuttered, seemingly caught off-guard, though he was a little surprised the leper had spotted – even known – his rank of major. 'Very kind of you.'

'Good, then I shall be gone,' the old man said. He shook his stave and the warning bells jingled. He started to shuffle forward once more on his wrecked, toeless, naked feet. Hastily the three of them got out of his way, for he seemed unable or unwilling to steer a course around them.

A few minutes later he was gone round the next bend and Nobby relaxed, while Irene held his hand tightly as if in need of reassurance. 'That was a turn up for the books, sir, eh?'

Nairs didn't reply. He was still wondering about the English leper's use of his rank. Finally he shook his head like a man trying to wake up from a deep sleep. He dismissed the strange apparition and said quietly, 'All right then, let's get cracking again. Move it.'

They moved it.

Behind the bend, the leper had paused. Chuckling a little crazily to himself, he removed the little metal shaving mirror from where he had hidden it in the folds of his dirty rags. He breathed on it. With difficulty he wiped it clean with his sleeve and then set about the business of signalling as they had told him to...

Seven

The little admiral flashed yet another glance at his wristwatch. Around him, Captain Leach and his senior staff officers tensed. Beneath their feet the steel trembled like a live thing as the turbines throbbed. It was as if the *Prince of Wales* was some kind of high-spirited animal, eager to be let off the leash.

Over at Cathay House, the highest building in Singapore, the single light flashed on and off three times. It was the signal. Almost immediately the first siren started to wail. It rose and fell and rose and fell again. It cut the stillness of the tropical afternoon like a crude obscenity uttered in polite company. One after another the other sirens took up the wail right across the island. The shrill cacophony cut into the busy evening life of the port as the planners had hoped it would.

Now the engineers stationed all around the naval base ignited their smoke pots. Thick black smoke started to mushroom into the still, blue-green evening sky. Almost instantly the base and the fleet of grey-painted warships began to disappear from the prying eyes on land. The little admiral flung a quick glance around the berth with his glasses. Apparently satisfied, he lowered them and nodded urgently to Captain Leach. He did the same and hurried away to the bridge telegraph.

A flight of aircraft started to cross the sky at a great height, but it was so cold up there that their contrails were clearly visible. Again the little admiral hoped that the watchers would be distracted from what was going on in the main naval basin. He wished that he could have asked the island's ack-ack gunners to fire a few dummy rounds at the flight of planes, as if they were really Japanese. But he knew that would be tempting fate. Some of Singapore's volunteers might have loaded and fired live ammo in their eagerness to get into the war.

Beneath his feet the deck trembled even more. He could hear the rattle of the great anchor chain running into the locker. Sailors were hurrying about their tasks. The most modern warship in the Royal Navy was being prepared and secured for night-running – blackout, the lot. He nodded, pleased. His sailors might be mostly H.O.

247

men, a goodly proportion of them not even yet twenty-one, but they were handling the 35,000 ton warship like veteran regulars.

The ship swung out of the main channel and started to proceed slowly to sea, hardly making any smoke, the little admiral noted with pleasure. Behind her came the *Repulse* and the destroyers. He lowered his glasses for the last time, praying that the trick had paid off – that no Jap spy had seen them go. For he knew instinctively – he felt it in his very bones almost – that the balloon was soon about to go up at Singapore.

Yet, even as he was pleased to see the end of their stay in Singapore, he was worried about the future. Instructions from the Admiralty in London were vague. It was clear, it appeared from their Lordships' decoding operations, that the little yellow men were on the high seas looking for trouble and it was also certain that they were going to attack both the British *and* the Americans. What *wasn't* clear was where those attacks would come in. So it meant that Force Z had thousands of square miles of ocean to patrol until the Japanese struck and all that they had to aid and protect them from Japanese attack was a mere eight aircraft – all antiquated seaplanes and decidedly very slow. One modern Jap fighter, flown by a bold pilot, would see them off in half an hour.

Now the great ships were beginning to gather speed. The wake behind them thrashed the muddy brown water into a frothy white. The admiral tried to relax, watching the shoreline go by as they emerged from the smoke screen. The European buildings had been replaced by the shoddy, tumble-down lean-tos of the locals. But as far as he could make out, no one in particular was watching the ships' passing. On the little sandy beach to port, there were a few skinny-legged, barefoot fishermen, repairing their nets, preparing their carbide lamps, lugging up sails from their huts, readying themselves for the night's fishing. But they didn't even look up at the ships. Perhaps, he told himself, they had seen too many naval vessels passing to and fro, going about their mysterious white business, which had absolutely no relevance to their own humble existence. The little admiral hoped so.

Captain Leach strode across the deck purposefully, like a man who enjoyed his work, though normally at this time of the day he would be in the wardroom enjoying a pre-dinner pink gin with his senior officers. 'Everybody stood to, sir,' he reported smartly.

'Good ... thanks, John. Well, what do you think?' He gave a vague wave of his hand, emcompassing everything – and nothing.

Captain Leach hesitated. He was uncertain, as he realized the admiral was. 'Well, sir,' he said slowly, 'I think we have done everything we could under the circumstances.'

'Yes, I suppose, we have,' the admiral agreed in a strange, faraway voice, as he realized that Leach was speaking in the past tense, as if their fate was decided already, and that this was the end of the road for them and their proud ships. He pulled himself together, shaking off the 'black dog', as Churchill always called it, the best he could, saying, 'See the chaps get their rum soon, John. We must not forget to splice the main brace.'

Leach forced a grin, trying to play the little admiral's game: two jolly upper-class naval officers who wouldn't even know danger, or perhaps disaster, if they saw it. 'England expects and all that sort of stuff, sir, what?'

'Yes,' the little admiral laughed shortly,

though there was no humour in the sound, 'England expects...'

Some fifteen miles away, as the sun finally sank behind the horizon and the heat of the day vanished abruptly as it always did in the tropics, Nairs told himself that with a bit of luck, they'd reach the Causeway by midnight; and that there there would surely be military transport to see them the rest of the way. For they were again about done. Indeed Nobby was half-carrying half-supporting the Chinese girl, Irene. Not that he minded it much, as weary as he was. He had taken quite a shine to her, Nairs had noticed with a fond smile. In the past Nobby had often declared he was a 'four-F' man – *find 'em, feel 'em, fuck 'em, and forget 'em'*. Now he was well and truly 'smitten', as he would have put it.

But despite the fact that they were close to their objective now, Nairs was careful. They had abandoned the road once more and were fighting their way through the vegetation that fringed it. For a while they had been making heavy weather through what Nairs had taken to be the usual mangrove swamp by the overpowering stink that came from it.

But eventually Nairs concluded they were really on the edge of some sort of stagnant lake from which thick coils of mist rose slowly into the humid air. There were naturally midges and mosquitoes everywhere and Nairs reasoned they'd all soon go down with malaria, now that they were not getting their daily dose of quinine. He consoled himself with the thought that they would not be much longer in the swamp.

As Nobby commented scornfully, 'Fancy, back home they pay good money to go to the flicks to see this kind of a thing. Sanders of the frigging River – no frigging thank you!' He hawked and spat angrily into the stagnant water.

The Chinese girl raised her weary head and began, 'Sanders – who–'

Nairs silenced her abruptly with an urgent, 'Quiet, Irene!'

They stopped as one. Now the only sound was the persistent, irritating croaking of the bullfrogs in the reeds around the lake. But another sound was beginning to impinge upon it – the soft shuffle of many feet and a faint sort of droning which only afterwards they recognized as some kind of dirge. Next to Irene, Nobby again felt the small hairs at the back of his shaven head begin to stand erect with fear. Irene gripped his hand more tightly and he knew that she, too, sensed impending danger.

Nairs, just a little way in front, crouched and tightened his hold on his weapon, as out of the night mist a line of eerie figures emerged, bent and slow, their heads enclosed by hoods so that they looked like a line of penitent monks from the Middle Ages. But it was not only the hooded figures which caught his attention. It was the big Sikhs – easy recognizable in their turbans and with their bushy beards carefully parted in the centre in the Sikh fashion – who were herding this strange group of weird individuals along, not hesitating to use their long staves or rifle butts if they were too slow for their guards.

Nairs screwed up his eyes and tried to penetrate the glowing gloom as they came closer and closer, the only sound the muffled curses of their guards and that which they made with their eerie shuffling through the dust on the road. He knew they were lepers – their previous encounter with the white one had alerted him to that. Now he could see, too, that these were of all races and colours. Mostly they were locals – Malays, naturally. But there was a big Sikh among them, another couple of white men, horribly disfigured, and one Negro, though how he got there, Nairs could not figure.

One thing, however, which he could figure was that these were former inmates of one of the isolated leper 'hospitals' in which they, the authorities, isolated such pathetic people. Now these Sikh rebels had released them from what in reality was a prison and were guiding them up-country. But to what purpose? These rebel Sikh police were not noted locally for their kindness. They were the feared policemen of the colony. Why should they aid these poor unfortunates who nobody wanted. Indeed if they dared to approach a local Malay kampong, they would be forced away with stones and dogs by the natives, terrified that they might catch the loathsome, body-wasting disease as well.

Then he had it. The Sikhs were using the lepers as a kind of weapon of war. The Sikhs knew, in that cheap cunning fashion of cops all over the world, that they would be no match for regular British troops, armed as they were solely with their rifles. But British soldiers were unused to lepers. They were terrified of any contact with them. What would they do if they found a bunch of them, blind, limbless, covered in great gaping ulcers and sores, wandering through their lines? Nairs knew the answer to that one immediately. They'd break and run; and that was exactly what the Sikhs had promised their new Japanese masters.

'Christ Almighty,' he whispered to himself. Urgently he relayed his suspicions to Nobby, as the dread procession came closer and closer, moving like wooden puppets, directed by some cruel, crazed puppetmaster who cared nothing about his creations, but was solely concerned with using them for his own evil purposes.

'Cor ferk a duck!' Nobby exclaimed wildly, when Nairs was finished. 'But what can we do about it?' He looked at his pathetic weapons. 'Not with this stick and my bondook. Can't stop the poor buggers with them.'

'I know ... I know,' Nairs agreed, his brain racing desperately as he sought for some solution.

Suddenly he had it. 'Have you got any matches, Nobby?' he asked.

'Course I have, sir. Need something to light my Woods, sir. All a poor old squaddie's got – his gaspers an'–'

'Shut up,' Nairs silenced his litany of woe

cruelly. 'The vegetation's all damp here in the jungle,' he explained. 'But that dead bamboo's still bone dry and if–'

'Got it, sir.' This time it was Nobby who did the interrupting. 'Light it and it'll go up like on Guy Fawkes night. That'll scatter the poor buggers. But what about the ruddy treacherous Sikhs?'

'Then we run like hell.' Nairs flashed a look at the girl in the darkness.

Irene nodded her head swiftly; she had understood the rapid interchange.

'All right, Nobby,' Nairs ordered, using one of the crudities that the little cockney corporal was fond of at moments like this. 'Don't hang around like a spare penis at a wedding. *Let's get cracking!*'

Nobby needed no urging. Although he had seen plenty of lepers in the years he had spent on the rubber plantation, they still frightened him. He wouldn't have touched one, as he had maintained many a time, '...if they paid me in ruddy gold sovereigns'. He struck the match. After a few moments there was a small flame. Hurriedly he shielded it with his hand. Slightly to his front, Nairs watched anxiously. But apparently none of the Sikhs had noticed the sudden tiny flame. Still they concentrated on driving the wretched lepers forward, some of them toiling up the road, supported by crude crutches, on virtually non-existent feet which had been reduced by the terrible wasting disease to mere stumps.

Nobby pulled up a handful of dry grass and applied another match to it. The grass burst into flame at once but Nobby hung on. When it started to scorch the small hairs at the back of his hand, he threw it into the bone-dry pile of bamboo.

With the force of a bomb exploding, it suddenly burst into flame. The bamboo crackled and hissed loudly. Nobby reeled back just in the time. The wall of fire shot forward. It advanced rapidly, devouring everything in front of it frighteningly, like a great blow-torch of flame, igniting more bamboo immediately.

A wild mêlée of screams, angry shouts and wild shooting commenced, as the captives and their captors came to a sudden halt, appalled by this abrupt wall of red flames that had erupted to their front. Nairs didn't give them a chance to recover from their shock. Standing up, firing wildly from the hip, he yelled at the top of his voice, as if he commanded scores of men, 'A *Company*

*rally on me ... B Company fire at will ... FIRE!
... C Company stand fast ... hold yer fire there,
man, I say...'*

Behind him Nobby did the same gleefully,
carried away by a wild lust for destruction,
while the Sikhs scattered, heading for the
undergrowth and the ditches, leaving their
poor pathetic charges wandering round in
panic-stricken groups, the blinded among
them holding their wasted arms in front of
their sightless eyes as if to ward off the
deadly flames.

It was a scene of almost medieval horror.
But the three fugitives had no time for
compassion. They knew their own lives were
at stake. Once the Sikhs had overcome their
panic and had rallied, they knew that they
wouldn't survive long. The big ex-
policemen would shoot them down like they
might have done some rabid village dog in
their previous role.

Nairs ripped off the rest of his magazine.
He didn't aim. It wasn't necessary. Most of
the Sikhs were cowering in the drainage
ditch on the opposite side of the road. In the
middle, the flames had now swirled round
their former captives. Two of them lay
burning furiously in the road, still moaning
weakly, but being reduced to the size of

charred pygmies by the intense heat. The rest were trying to escape. But at the pace they could move, most of the poor pathetic creatures were flame-bound already, with one native woman trying to beat the flames that were burning her flaccid breasts with her stumps of hands.

'Come on ... come on, for God's sake,' Nairs called thickly, knowing that he would begin to vomit if he had to see much more of this horror – he could already feel the hot bile flooding his throat. 'Let's get the hell out of here!'

The other two had had enough as well. Irene was sobbing openly and Nobby was muttering foul obscenities under his breath, as if he could not stand the horrible sight any longer and was attempting to make it vanish by the power and strength of his curses.

They broke off the wild firefight. With Nairs in the lead and a protective Nobby holding on to the sobbing Chinese girl to his rear, they pushed into the fringing jungle, blundering by a leper fighting off the flaming foliage with a crude crutch. But his struggles were getting weaker by the instant. Already the stumps of his feet were beginning to char a flaky black. It looked horrific, but Nairs knew he felt no pain. In an instant, when his stumps had burned away, he would tumble to the ground. Nairs wished he could have shot him. But there was no time if they were going to save themselves.

They pushed on.

Bullets cut the foliage to their right. 'Christ,' Nobby cried, 'the buggers have spotted us.' He yelled in sudden pain as a slug nipped at his bare upper arm. Blood spurted out in a red arc immediately. Still he knew enough to keep on running. Anyone who fell out now wouldn't live long.

'Pigs of Englishmen!' The great angry roar came from their right. A Sikh, minus his turban so that his long oiled hair hung down from beneath his comb like that of a woman, came charging at them, bayonet fixed. Nairs had no time to use his rifle – the magazine was empty anyway. Instead he thrust it up to the parry position. The two rifles slammed together. Nairs felt an electric shock fly up his arms. For one terrible moment he thought he was going to drop his rifle, but he didn't.

With all his energy, he clashed with the Sikh, forcing his bayonet to one side, but not losing contact, for the native policeman was too powerful for him to do that. Instead the latter yelled with triumph, brought up his bayonet from below. Obviously he was a trained bayonet fighter, for he tried to slip his bayonet under and up to force Nairs to lose his grip on his own rifle.

But those years of his youth when he had fought man-to-man in a life-and-death struggle in the trenches paid off. Nairs was a fraction of a second quicker than the Sikh. His butt rammed downwards. It caught the other man completely by surprise. He breathed out, a rapidly deflating balloon, as the cruel butt caught him in his mighty belly. He started to crumple, blood trickling out of the side of his gaping mouth. Nairs didn't give him a chance to recover. 'Take that, you big bastard!' he yelled through gritted teeth and rammed the brass-shod butt of his Lee Enfield up and straight into the Sikh's teeth. He screamed shrilly and went reeling back. Nairs sprang over him, kicking him cruelly under his bearded chin as he did. There was a brittle click like a dry twig snapping underfoot in a hot summer. The Sikh's head lolled to one side. He was unconscious or dead, Nairs neither knew nor cared. Next moment all three of them were running for their lives...

Eight

It was shortly after nine o'clock that Saturday evening. At Chequers, forty-five miles north of London, Clementine Churchill had gone to bed early. She wasn't feeling well – stomach upset; it often was – and she had left Winston to deal with his important guests alone. But that was nothing new. Her husband was really very Victorian. He liked to dine with his men guests without women, as was the nineteenth-century custom. She supposed they could talk more freely about the things that seemed to interest men, boring things like money, war, politics, perhaps even loose women, that way.

Now Churchill dined with his two important guests, emphasizing time and time again the fact that he, himself, was half American, for both of them were American: Roosevelt's special envoy, Averell Harriman, who one day, surprisingly enough, would marry his daughter-in-law Pamela; and John Winant, the new US ambassador, who had just succeeded that crook and traitor, with his pro-Nazi leanings, Joe Kennedy.

They had just finished the main course, with Churchill toying with the meat, for he was more interested in the drink and the wines than the food, when the butler tapped discreetly on the door and entered.

Churchill, who never noticed servants really, but deigned now and again to acknowledge his chief one, asked, 'Well, what is it, Saunders?'

The middle-aged butler looked suitably grave. 'Sir, we have just heard the Home Service nine o'clock news.' Suddenly he appeared very flustered, as if he had suddenly realized his master night well be very upset by what he had to say.

Churchill prompted. 'Well Saunders, what have you heard on the Home Service nine o'clock news?'

But irony was wasted on the butler at that particular moment. 'One of the footmen caught it, sir, when I went out for – er – my evening glass of stout.'

The three of them were amused by the butler; it was almost as if he were one of those caricatures of an English servant current in the popular wartime movies from Hollywood, where they evidently thought that all English people of a certain class lived in great Elizabethan houses, surrounded by servants and, naturally, rose gardens.

'And?'

Saunders hesitated, as if he had come to announce that the cook had 'had one of her turns' due to an excessive consumption of her favourite tipple, gin. 'He heard, sir, as did the other members of the staff in the kitchen,' Saunders pulled a face as if this hurt him personally, 'that Japan has attacked the Americans at a place – er – called Pearl Harbor, sir. That's what they heard.'

There was a moment of absolute, total silence, broken only by the lonely hoot of an owl in the skeletal trees outside. It was almost as if Saunders had dropped a bomb personally and wiped them all out. Suddenly, startlingly, Churchill jumped to his feet with the alacrity of a man half his age. 'We shall declare war on Japan *forthwith*,' he declared stoutly, as the two Americans stared at each other incredulously.

'I shall go to my office and place a call to your President immediately,' Churchill added, looking as if he were definitely pleased at the sombre news. That statement woke the dark-haired, saturnine US ambassador from his daze at the news that the USA might well be at war for the second time in a quarter of a century. 'Don't you think you'd better get confirmation first, sir?' he asked. 'You don't declare war on the strength of a radio announcement, PM.'

But Churchill wasn't listening. He knew that terrible things were going to happen now that Japan had entered the war so dramatically. There would be sore defeats, great losses of men and material. But even as he dismissed those sombre thoughts, hurrying to his office to call Roosevelt and pledge Britain's support in the new war against Japan, he knew, We have won ... we *have won after all...*

In his dotage when he recalled that day, his half-mad eyes would fill with tears. But they were never tears of regret and sorrow; they were shed in gratitude and thanksgiving...

Now they knew they had almost reached the Causeway. There were Indian troops with their British officers everywhere, extending the defences, placing new strong-points and posts for their antiquated Lewis guns. A very weary Nairs told himself that judging by their fanlike turbans, which their white officers also wore, they were Rajputs – dark, slim men with beautiful white smiles, who waved to the three bedraggled fugitives as they trudged by, with one of them, obviously a cook – he was fatter than the rest of his fellow infantrymen – waving a freshly baked chapatti at them, as if offering them it to eat.

They shook their heads and forced themselves to return his brilliant smile. It was good to be back with their own people again. Soon they would pass on to Intelligence what they knew and Nairs, for one, knew he'd sleep for days on end. No food, no drink, nothing but sleep to heal his exhausted, torn body and make him forget the horrors of the past week.

So they moved on, the estuary of the Straits a glistening silver snake a mile to their front. There was the clipclop of horse's hooves. Even in their fazed state, the noise startled then. Not many people save the really rich kept horses in Malaya. Naturally the natives didn't have any; horses were confined to imported polo ponies, mainly, belonging to the nabobs who could afford them and their Indian grooms and syces.

They stopped as the rider approached them. He was an old man with the handlebar moustache of the Victorian age. He was wearing some kind of uniform, too, ablaze with medal ribbons and on his shoulders he had chainmail epaulettes of the kind Nairs hadn't seen for many years. Nairs and Nobby Clark came to attention and saluted weakly. 'Morning, Brigadier,' they said as one, recognizing his rank and wondering where a brigadier, wearing a revolver and carrying an old-fashioned cavalry sword was off to this fine December morning.

The Brigadier touched his solar topee with a wrinkled, gnarled old hand, covered with liver spots. 'Mornin',' he quavered in a reedy voice. He had to be at least eighty, Nairs thought. 'Any sign of 'em?'

'Sign, sir?'

'The little yellow men, Major,' the Brigadier replied testily, as if it was the most obvious thing in the world. 'Everyone's got to do his bit. Or we're in for a damned fine bloody nose, what?'

'Yessir,' Nairs agreed hesitantly. 'The Japs, sir–'

'Yes, the damned impertinent devils have landed at last up on the coast. Personally been expecting it for weeks. Now it's every hand to the tiller, what, now they've gone.'

'Gone, sir–' But already the mad old man in his Boer War uniform was urging his horse forward, as if he couldn't get to the scene of battle hastily enough.

Nobby stared at Nairs and scratched his beard. 'That's a turn-up for the books, sir,' he exclaimed. 'Wonder what he meant by "now they've gone".'

Nairs shrugged with feigned carelessness. 'Search me,' he answered, though he was already being overcome with dread as if he already half-realized what had happened. They plodded on.

The stream of refugees, with their pathetic bits and pieces tied up in bundles carried on their heads, had dried up now. Perhaps the guards lining the road, recruited from the Singapore Home Guard, had intimidated them. Now there was relative silence. Even the noise from the shipyards and the crews of the old coastal tubs which plied their trade on the Straits and the outlying islands was absent. It was as if Singapore, which usually came to life so early, was still asleep.

Nobby looked at one of the Chinese home guards who was tucking into his traditional pork and noodles, plying his chopsticks with amazing speed. But the cockney's eyes were not on the steaming hot food bought from a kiosk further down the approach road, they were fixed almost hypnotically on the dripping bottle of ice-cold Chinese beer resting on the log next to where he was seated. 'Cor!' he muttered to himself, 'I could sink half a dozen o' them and not even notice.'

Irene, who had recovered from her night's ordeal, pressed his hand happily. 'My grandfather in Singapore – he rich. He buy shopful beer,' she chirped.

Nairs grinned to himself, as they came down the incline to the Straits. He knew Nobby fancied the Chinese girl, despite the difference in their ages. Perhaps it might work out and he'd soon have a nice, fat Chink grandfather-in-law. Nobby deserved it, though he wondered how Irene would go down in the Mile End Road.

They turned the bend in the descent and there it was on the other side of the Straits – the naval anchorage. And it was totally, completely, empty. There wasn't a single Royal Naval vessel there, except the normal bumboat manned by an auxiliary Chinese crew, which cleared up the anchorage after the larger ships of the South China station had left. The matelots of the fleet called it, in an apt description of its function, 'HMS Shitsweeper'.

'They've gone,' Nobby gasped and sat down on the bank abruptly, as if someone had punched him in his skinny guts and knocked all the air out of him. The girl dropped down to his side and patted his hand gently as if comforting him.

For a moment or two Nairs was too shocked to speak. After all they had been through, trying to reach Singapore with the vital information... Now it was just too late. They had missed the two great ships that they had struggled so hard to save.

Nobby looked up at him. 'Er, what now brown cow–' he began as he realised the overwhelming seriousness of this moment and his voice lost its old bantering tone. 'What?' he asked lamely.

Again Nairs looked at that bare stretch of dirty water, with the refuse of the departed fleet bobbing up and down in it, while the crew of 'HMS Shitsweeper' tried to fish it out with their nets and dredges. He shrugged and put his hands in his pockets, shoulders hunched like a man defeated. 'Come on,' he said, not answering Nobby's question. 'Let's see if we can get a ride across the Causeway in one of those Army three-tonners. There's nothing we can do now, is there?'

Nobby said, 'Suppose yer right, sir.' He turned to Irene while Nairs started to trudge to where a small convoy of three-ton lorries waited for their turn to cross the Straits into a doomed Singapore. 'Come on, girl,' he added tonelessly.

'Nobby, I come,' she answered willingly enough.

On another occasion he would have made a rude comment on that statement. But not now. He had no spirit left.

Down below the Tommies waiting in the trucks in the burning heat were making sheep-like noises and singing tunelessly, *'Oh why are we waiting ... why are we waiting...'*

Book Four: Defeat

One

'Up periscope,' Commander Harada, the commander of *L-165*, ordered.

The petty officer in his beribboned cap pressed the electric button. There was the hiss of escaping compressed air. The shining slick tube of steel rose rapidly. Click. It came to a stop and fastened hard.

Harada spun his cap round. Now it was back to front with the peak to the rear. The little Japanese submarine skipper looked a little absurd in the cap now, but no one commented on the fact. The skipper had a sharp temper, and was inclined to threaten to use the samurai sword he wore, even in the narrow, hot confines of the sub, at the slightest provocation. No, Harada was not a man to be trifled with.

It was three days now since the Imperial

Japanese Army had begun landing troops on the east coast of the Malay Peninsula and they had been successful everywhere, save at the British-held beach at Kota Bharu. Now it was *L-165's* task to ensure that no British surface craft interfered with the success of those landings, especially the new one planned at Kota Bharu beach. That was why Harada had stationed his craft between the beach and Singapore, some 400 miles north of the great British port.

Harada peered through the circle of calibrated glass. A ship slid silently into the gleaming light, neatly dissected by the range-finding lines. He cursed to himself, while around in the green-glowing light, his half-naked, bearded, sweating crew waited expectantly for his verdict. He turned up the amplifier. The ship shot in a flash much closer. Again the tough little Japanese submarine captain cursed. He was still out of range and now he could see another and much larger warship sliding into the circle of glass. Hastily he sang out. 'Identification book.'

Next to him, his second-in-command thrust the book into his free hand. Ironically enough it was one prepared by a British publishing house, *Jane's Fighting Ships*.

273

Without looking down, Harada thumbed through the well-used pages until he came to the section he knew by feel alone dealt with British warships.

He peered through the periscope, noting the ship's superstructure and the unusual arrangement of its big guns. Yes, it had to be, he told himself. He flashed a look at the silhouettes on the page of the identification book. 'Yes,' he said to himself, 'it's her.'

'Which ship, sir?' his second-in-command asked excitedly. He could see in the book that it was a capital ship. What a triumph it would be, if on their first combat mission against the arrogant round eyes they could sink one of their major warships, he told himself, hardly able to conceal his excitement.

'*Prince of Wales,*' Commander Harada said, 'I'm one hundred per cent certain of that.'

'Action stations ... we attack, sir?'

Harada didn't reply. Instead he fiddled with the dials of the rangefinder attached to the periscope.

The waiting crew hardly dared breathe. Now there was no sound, save that of the skipper's heavy breathing, the purr of the electric motors and the steady drip-drip of a leak somewhere or other in the boat.

Furiously Harada whirled the dials. The *Prince of Wales* sprang into even greater focus, despite the bad weather raging up top.

Harada's second-in-command couldn't contain himself any longer, his nerves were running away with him. He risked Harada's famous temper by asking again, 'Well, sir, action stations?'

Harada swung round at him, face savage, dark eyes blazing furiously. 'No, dammit! she's out of damned range...'

Force Z had been saved – unwittingly – for the first time. But not for long. Now the airwaves over the Far East were buzzing with coded messages zipping back and forth. A frustrated and very angry Commander Harada had naturally reported the sighting of the *Prince of Wales* and the rest of Force Z. He had given the British fleet's position, course and bearing north of Singapore.

Immediately the Japanese admirals ceased the celebrations of their great victory over the American Fleet at Pearl Harbor. They forgot their sake and were sober immediately as they realized this new danger. It was obvious what the round eyes intended. The British were going to interfere with the vital landings on the Malay peninsula. Once they got among the undefended troop transports with their great cannon, the Japanese infantry preparing for the second attack on the beach at Kota Bharu would be slaughtered mercilessly. Their initial victory in Malaya might well yet turn into defeat.

At three on the afternoon of 10 December, the Japanese HQ in Malaya received a second report from another submarine that the British squadron was now steering south. At once all Japanese submarines were ordered to surface and take up the pursuit of the British at full speed. The British ships had to be sunk regardless of the cost.

While the surfaced Japanese subs battled southwards in ever-worsening weather, the entire Japanese naval force under the command of Admiral Nobutake Kondo, consisting of the battleships *Kongo* and *Haruna,* and one cruiser squadron, plus one of destroyers, was ordered to leave its stations protecting the landings. Despite the Japanese admiral's protests that he was no match for the round eyes, he was told to engage the *Wales* and *Repulse.* As some sort of consolation he was informed by his superiors that he stood a good chance of

276

inflicting damage on the superior British ships in a night action.

By late afternoon, however, Admiral Kondo lost contact. Now a desperate Commander Harada took a chance. Surfacing, his little boat rocking frantically in the high swell, the little Japanese sub commander resighted Force Z. It was at extreme range. Still Harada knew he had to attempt a second attack. He wouldn't get another chance, he knew that.

With their yellow faces glistening with sweat, as if they had been rubbed in grease, the crew of the *L-165* tensed over their instruments and weapons, Many of them were clad only in G-strings or loincloths. Bearded and naked, bathed in the red gleam of the attack lighting, they looked like savages, totally out of place in this mass of modern technology. But they were all highly trained, specialists to a man. They knew exactly what they were about.

Now in reply to the skipper's demands, they reported their stations, *'Torpedo tubes one to four ... closed up, sir ... Aft torpedo tubes ... five to nine ... closed up, sir...'*

'Bearing green-one ... zero,' Number One sang out. He had spotted the leading ship of the enemy force, ploughing through the

heaving grey sea.

Harada wasted no more time. 'Periscope down,' he snapped. A rush, a metallic slither and the gleaming polished tube came hissing down. He waited, counting off the seconds, his mind already racing with the technical details of the attack soon to come. 'Take her up,' he ordered.

There was a bubbling hiss of more compressed air leaving the tanks. Now the submarine was much higher in the water. It was risky, Harada knew. But he'd risk it. He wanted a clear shot with a fan of at least four torpedoes at the round eyes' force.

Hastily the conning tower hatch was unscrewed. Freezing seawater poured into the sub, drenching the gun crew gathered below, waiting for orders to man the deck gun if it was necessary.

Harada ignored the water and the howling wind. He yelled an order through the voice tube, the wind snatching the words from his mouth. The submarine began to swing round with damnable slowness, fighting the powerful current. Harada bent to the powerful binoculars, attached to the lip of the conning tower, and peered through them. He glimpsed a ship momentarily. Then she dipped and disappeared into a great heaving trough. But he knew the round eyes were still there. Now he pointed the sub at the unseen ship, as if it were the weapon. 'Stand by tubes,' he called.

'Standing by,' the disembodied voice from below came up to him.

The Japanese skipper hesitated only long enough to say a quick prayer. Next moment, he yelled, 'Fire ... *one through four!*'

A hiss. A flurry of escaping air bubbles to left and right. The sub heaved. Suddenly lightened by the weight of one-ton tubes of sudden violent death flashing from her innards, she was momentarily out of control. Harada ignored the fact. His dark eyes gleamed with almost unbearable excitement, as he stared at his stopwatch, counting off the seconds. *'One ... two ... three...'* He knew that if he didn't hear the hollow boom of steel striking steel by five, he would have missed. *'Four ... five...'* His voice broke ... *Nothing.'* He had missed or they were out of range.

From below came the frantic voice of Number One. 'Anything to report, Commander ... anything ...?' He turned the switch and the intercom went dead. Slowly tears started to trickle down his hard yellow face. He had failed...

'Did I ever tell yer about the tart with the two sets of tits,' Big Slack Arse was saying as the two old 'stripeys' lingered over their cocoa. Elsewhere, the off-duty men were unslinging their hammocks, rubbing their feet, cleaning their toenails with their jackknives, picking their noses and staring at nothing, – the hundred and one boring things that made up a sailor's life on so-called 'active service'. Not one of them talked about the near miss with the 'tin fish' which had appeared out of nowhere and had then begun to drift purposelessly, as they ran out of juice.

'Yes,' his running mate Little Slack Arse answered a little wearily. 'But you *will*, that you *will!*' He said the words without rancour. Mates had to stick together in the Royal Navy even when they'd heard each other's tales a dozen times over. You never knew when you'd need a good oppo.

Big Slack Arse cleared the last of the hard wax from his ear, glanced at the brown deposit on the end of his forefinger as if it was of some importance to do so, cleared his throat and commenced, 'Well, it was back in thirty-eight at Pompey, like. I's just got my first badge up and was due a little extra pay, like, so I thought to mesen–'

'That I'd go out on the town, have a couple of pints and see what the juicy Lucys was doing...' his mate mimicked him cruelly. 'Get on with it,' he added, 'Get to the dirty bit where she offered to give yer something new for yer frigging ten bob.'

Big Slack Arse was in no way offended. It was his nature never to take things too seriously. That's why he was a stripey still after nearly nineteen years in the Royal Navy. 'Well, as I was saying before I was rudely interrupted by somebody who shall remain nameless, I thought I'd go down to Pompey and get mesen a bit o' the other with the extra pay, like. And I'd had just had a jar or two in the old Bottle and Cock. Yer know, the pub that bought it last year in the Blitz where–'

'Where they found the frigging landlord, still holding a double whisky in his frigging hand with his frigging legs sawn off at the knees.'

'Christ on a crutch,' Big Slack Arse exclaimed in surprise, 'how did *you* know all that?'

'Because you frigging well told me – Oh, get on with it.'

'Oh ay. Well I started chatting up this here

juicy Lucy. She weren't much to look at. Face like a dog's dinner to be frank. But she had plenty in her jumper, I can tell yer that. Yer'd have said she had a couple of tons of melons up there. Well, using me old charm – it's not for nothing that they used to call me the Rudolph Valentino of Pompey back in the old days–'

'Get frigging on with it!'

'Oh all right. So I sez to her, right witty, like, if you show me yours, I'll show yer mine. And yer know what she sez? Sailor, I'll show yer something that'll make yer frigging glassy orbs pop outa their sockets. And she hauls up her jumper. She didn't have a vest on underneath, like, and there they were – two rows of 'em.' He smiled hugely.

'Yer mean tits?'

'That I do,' Big Slack Arse said proudly, as if he had achieved something of significance. 'And they wasn't little 'uns like them filum stars have either. These were real *tits*, big juicy *tits*, *tits* with knobs on 'em, *tits* like what yer could get your choppers into, *tits* that was too good for nippers, *tits*–'

'Will you stop talking about *tits!*' his running mate cried in exasperation, 'and get to the mucky part, for Chrissake.'

But that was not fated to be. Just as the

older stripey opened his mouth to explain to what unusual use he had put the 'tits', the ship's tannoy crackled into noisy, metallic noise. 'Air raid ... air raid...' the warning came through, 'All duty men stand at their duty stations ... all off-watch men, be prepared for action stations as well ... Air raid ... air raid...'

'Holy mother of God,' Little Slack Arse moaned, 'Is there no frigging rest for the frigging wicked?'

Apparently there wasn't...

Captain Tennant of the *Repulse*, had just enjoyed a hearty breakfast of coffee, cold ham, bread and coffee and had clambered up to the bridge, when first contact was made. *'Aircraft approaching fast!'* the alarmist signal came up from the radar room and immediately the crew was ordered to action stations. In controlled confusion, the gunners rushed to their turrets in their coveralls, gloves, anti-flash hoods, helmets. Down below as the deck prepared for action, with the duty pilot already seated in his Walrus, the engine running, waiting for the command to take off on what might well be a one-way mission, the surgeon lieutenant and his medics prepared their gleaming instruments for the expected casualties. Further below the cooks dowsed the galley fires, while the hooded firecrews stood by for the first blaze. Everywhere a sense of confident, tense urgency reigned.

On the flag deck, Captain Tennant searched the grey, overcast, tropical sky. Nothing. That pleased him. He called into the voice tube. 'First sign of enemy aircraft, let me know *at once,* Jones.'

The radar officer, a pedantic Welshman, ideal for the job, answered in the affirmative, as Tennant turned to his Number One, saying, 'I'd say we're for it, Guy. No air cover and none that could reach us in time if the little yellow fellers hit us before we reach the cover of the shore for whatever good that might do us.'

His second-in-command tried to cheer up the commander of the great battlecruiser with 'We're staying in formation all right, sir...' he indicated the destroyers about a mile or so to each side of the *Repulse* 'and the shore is coming up fast. And that looks like an island in front of us.' He focused his glasses and the skipper of the *Repulse* did the same, telling himself that land wasn't the best of cover. But it was better than the open sea when attacked by enemy dive-bombers. He'd experienced that often enough in the Med the previous year. 'Suppose you're–' he commenced, but was interrupted by the shrill peep from the flag deck's voice tube.

Swiftly he grabbed the antiquated instrument, pulled out the chained plug and blew down it, saying, 'Captain here.'

'Sir.' It was Jones, his Welsh accent more pronounced than ever. In the wardroom the other junior officers often made fun of it and his being 'a boyo from the valleys', in what they fondly supposed was a Welsh accent.

'Yes.'

'We're being shadowed sir ... to port.'

Hastily the two senior officers flung up their glasses and focused them. They *were* being shadowed. They could see the slow-moving dark spot of the plane some two miles or so away, quite clear in the bright red of the sun which hung on the glittering horizon as if it were too weak to rise any further.

'Mitsubishi 196,' his Number One announced.

'Jap naval service?'

'Exactly, sir. Their surface ships are on to us.'

'Shit!' Tennant exclaimed. 'That's torn it.'

His Number One said nothing. He knew only too well what was going on. If they were being shadowed by a Japanese naval plane, it meant their navy was involved, and if the Jap Fleet, intent on attacking them, contained an aircraft carrier, then – he didn't think that particular unpleasant thought to its logical conclusion. Instead he gazed at the destroyers, wondering at their grey, knifelike beauty, as they cleaved through the pea-green sea, slicing it into twin bright-white curls...

As yet the little admiral, whose ship had unwittingly dodged the four torpedoes fired at it by Commander Harada, had seen no sign of the bombers predicted by his own radar. It was not unusual. The radar sets were not that accurate. Often threats of impending action reported by the hard-pressed, sweating operators perched in front of their green-glowing dials turned out to be shoals of fish or flights of migrating birds. So now he concentrated on what was happening on the shore about a mile away where the Japanese were supposed to have landed. He had already dispatched the destroyer *Express* to do a recce. Now he opened the signal from the *Express's* captain with fingers that trembled slightly to read the latter's message, while the signaller waited attentively at his side with his message pad at the ready.

The message gave him a sense of relief as he read through it hastily. With the humour that senior officers expected – sometimes – from destroyer skippers in their mid-twenties, the *Express's* captain reported: 'Enemy vanished. All as quiet as a wet Sunday afternoon.'

The little admiral turned to the waiting rating. 'All right, Sparks, signal, message received. Investigate further. Thanks.'

Swiftly the man wrote it down and disappeared below decks to send the message, while the little admiral beamed at no one in particular, feeling that a load had been lifted from his skinny shoulders for a while at least. To the south-east, the Japanese reconnaissance plane continued to circle and circle silently. But the little admiral did not see their 'shadow'. It wouldn't have mattered now if he had...

They approached the Emperor, crossing the Throne Room as if they were crawling, hair shaven to their yellow skulls, breathing loudly through their nostrils in a sign of respect. Behind them the generals and admirals of the Imperial General Staff trailed their overlong traditional swords absurdly. Indeed there was something absurd about the whole business: the chamberlains in their striped pants and frock coats, although it was only eight in the morning here in Tokyo; the guards in their medieval costumes, and the Emperor himself, bespectacled and weedy looking, for all the world more like a humble bank clerk than the divine ruler of the Imperial Japanese Empire.

They were all hard, tough men, hardened even more by the long cruel campaign in China. Military men that they were, they still ran everything from the Japanese Imperial Diet to the great industrial firms, such as Datsun and Mitsubishi. All the same, they had respect enough for the Emperor, who was happiest playing with his botanical specimens and wondering how he could produce a second male heir to the Imperial throne without resorting to a concubine, to seek his permission for what they intended off Malaya, now the shooting war they had wished for so fervently had finally commenced.

General Tojo, soon to be the virtual dictator of the country, bald-headed, bespectacled and buck-teethed, spoke for them. Apparently hardly daring to raise himself, he addressed the God on the raised dais in front of him, never elevating his gaze higher than Hirohito's chin. 'If we now sink the British fleet off Malaya,' he hissed, 'then we might face yet another problem with Russia.'

The Divine Being waved his fan as if to indicate that Tojo should explain. They had been having trouble with Russia ever since Japan had invaded Manchuria back in the early thirties. What could the Russians want this time?

'His Imperial Majesty, in all his infinite wisdom knows that Russia is under severe pressure from our German allies,' Tojo said, trying in no way to lecture Hirohito; that would amount to blasphemy almost. 'But the Russians still have a formidable army in the East. If we occupy ourselves completely in this way, withdrawing troops from China and using the mass of our air and naval forces, his Imperial Majesty knows that the Russians might use the opportunity to attack us in our state of weakness.' He finished abruptly and lowered his shaven head once more like some miserably broken-down coolie, as he waited for Emperor Hirohito to make his decision.

There was a heavy silence, save for the muffled tone of a gong beating somewhere. Closer by, the waiting generals and admirals, big rumps sticking up absurdly, could hear the childish laughter of the heir to the Imperial throne, Akihito, playing some game or other. It was obviously not the right game, for a female voice was chiding him in the special Imperial language, which few of the commoners present could really understand. After all it was reserved for noble courtiers and members of the royal family.

After what seemed a long time, Hirohito cleared his throat mildly. They raised their heads ever so slightly, like cautious soldiers peering hesitantly over a trench parapet, prepared to have them blown off by some lurking enemy. He said just one word: *'Hai'* (yes).

It was sufficient. The Divine Spirit had agreed to the bombing. The fate of Force Z was finally sealed...

The *Repulse's* loudspeakers crackled into urgent action. *'Enemy aircraft approaching ...*

aircraft approaching,' they warned dramatically... *'ACTION STATIONS!'*

Again the ship's complement raced to their posts. They were fast and silent. Most of them wore rubber gym shoes on their feet. Others, on account of the heat, had donned rugby and football jerseys to cover their skins against flames. They looked like a multi-coloured third-class soccer team as they charged to their positions.

Nine aircraft in perfect formation, outlined a stark sinister black against the perfect blue sky, headed towards them. The anti-aircraft gunners craned their necks and shaded their eyes, waiting for the order to open fire. At the rangefinders, the ratings called out the range, ever decreasing now, in quiet, orderly voices. The Senior Service was living up to its reputation of never panicking. All was calm, controlled caution now. It wouldn't be long.

Then there it was. With startling suddenness, the order rang out. 'All units – *OPEN FIRE ... FIRE, FIRE, FIRE...'*

Soon the sky was flecked by brown patches and criss-crossed by the lethal lines of burning red-and-white tracer. Majestically the Japanese dive-bomber squadron steered through the anti-aircraft fire. It was as if nothing could stop them.

Down below the gunners fired and fired. They swung their quick-firing Bofors around. Gleaming, smoking shell cases tumbled to the deck in metallic profusion. The hoists bringing up the ammunition worked full out. Brawny gunlayers cradled shells to their chests like deadly babies.

The first bomber was hit. It seemed to stagger in mid-air, as if it had abruptly run into a brick wall. For what seemed an age nothing happened. Then with dramatic suddenness, its left wing fell off. Like a great metallic leaf it started to sail round and round to the sea far below. Next moment the crippled plane fell out of the sky, roaring downwards, trailing behind it a great cherry-red blowtorch of furious flame.

The sweating gunners cheered madly. Not for long. The destruction of that first plane seemed to act like a signal. The formation split, as if to some unspoken command. They peeled to left and right. Some hovered there like great metal hawks. Others prepared to attack.

The first plane flung itself out of the sky. With a great roar it came howling down. Immediately, at the command of the gunnery control officer, the *Repulse's* gunners concentrated on the single plane seemingly dicing with death.

Down and down it came hurtling. Now, it seemed, as if it never would be able to pull out its death-defying dive. On the bridge Captain Tennant, watching its progress, focused on the dark outline of a head in the gleaming perspex of the Jap plane's canopy; he could imagine the pilot pressed against his seat with the 'G' force, his face flattened like a pancake against his bones. He clenched his fists and willed him not to come out of his dive.

The bomber broke at the very last minute. In the same instant that Tennant yelled *'He's in the bloody drink!'* the Japanese pilot pulled out of that death-defying dive. Deadly black eggs tumbled in crazy profusion from the plane's blue-black belly. Suddenly everything was noise, explosion, crazy. The bombs straddled the great ship. Huge founts of water shot up, higher than the superstructure. A radio mast, sliced in half by razor-sharp shrapnel, came tumbling down in a jumble of wire and twisted steel, angry blue electric sparks flying everywhere.

Now the *Repulse's* ordeal commenced in earnest. Plane after plane zipped at four hundred miles an hour through the steel network of exploding anti-aircraft shells. Sweating, shirts black with moisture, the gunners swung their weapons round furiously. Their feet seemed to be disappearing into a mound of steaming brass cartridges and shell cases. Time and time again the great ship rocked with near misses. All the same she seemed to bear a charmed life as she zig-zagged crazily, tearing up a mad wake of boiling white water as she tried to avoid her fate.

Abruptly the whole massive ship trembled. She had been hit. A single Japanese bomb had fallen on a hangar, pierced it and exploded on a mess deck below. The bomb exploded with a mighty roar. Men screaming frantically, ran back and forth, their limbs burning furiously, weakening by the moment as the cruel flames devoured their flesh, charring it a crumbly black, leaving the bare bones to gleam like polished ivory.

The fire parties went into action at once. Bravely they fought the raging inferno, forcing it back, as it spluttered and spattered in the streams of seawater. It was almost like some defiant wild beast, trapped in its lair, fighting to the inevitable end.

Then they had it out. Tennant increased

the speed of the *Repulse* as the moaning casualties from below were laid out on the deck, waiting for the medics to attend to them. The dead were simply covered with blankets, ready to be consigned to the deep, once order was re-established.

The blanketing out of the fire seemed to act as a signal for the Japanese. As abruptly as they had appeared, the survivors turned, closed formation and began to wing their way back to their bases in Indo-China, leaving behind them a loud echoing silence which seemed to go on for ever.

An overjoyed Tennant heightened his speed even further. At a steady twenty-five knots, its proud prow cleaving the waves effortlessly, the *Repulse* plunged on...

The little admiral was overjoyed too. They had fought their first battle. As one-sided as it had been in the favour of the Japanese airmen, the little force of Royal Navy ships had triumphed. At that moment he would have dearly loved to have ordered 'Splice the mainbrace!' His crews certainly deserved a good portion of 'Pusser's grog', as even the H.O. men had learned to call it. But there was no time for that now. They had to reach the shelter of the shore before the little yellow men jumped them once more, which they would. *They had to!*

The minutes passed by, while the men on the gundecks relaxed. Cooks passed among them, as they did so, doling out tea from the great steaming, polished dixies, handing those who wanted them giant bully beef sandwiches, though the men were generally too parched to swallow them. They weren't allowed to smoke on the gundeck, so they were given boiled sweets and the like, despite the protests of the older hands that 'Yer'd frigging think we was frigging schoolbairns – givin' us gobstoppers like this!' Still, even the old hands were glad of the respite and more than once, although they feigned bored toughness, they eyed the ever-closer shoreline almost with a kind of longing which said, 'For Chrissake get us there, Tom Thumb. Give a poor ole matelot a frigging bit o' cover.'

That wasn't to be. The Japanese had scented blood. These pilots were the cream of the Japanese Air Force – most of them would be dead before the year was out. Now their honour was at stake. Even if they were to return to Japan in an urn, they would return in honour. So it was that the next formation of dive-bombers came surging in from the sun. They had adopted the German attack tactic, rising up and down, flying in some cases at wave-top height to put the defending gunners off their aim, even lowering their undercarriage in a daring attempt to decrease their speed and make it even more difficult for the round-eye gunners to draw a bead on them.

The gunnery officers reacted at once as the klaxons sounded the alert. *'ACTION STATIONS!'* they roared, red-faced and angry. *'FIRE ... FIRE ... FIRE!'* The cooks in their dirty aprons dropped their canteens and dixies and ran for it as the guns opened up with an earsplitting roar, the machine-guns chattering frantically, sending up a seemingly solid wall of furious white tracer.

Big Slack Arse seized his opportunity. He'd been waiting for the next alert for quite a while. He'd even neglected the 'NAAFI bangers' that Little Slack Arse had purchased as a special treat – unknown to both of them as they wolfed the special sausages down, the grease trickling down their chins, these would be the last 'bangers and beans' they'd ever eat. He nipped through the open door of the purser's store with surprising speed for such a big fat man. A bottle of the 'Pusser's rum' disappeared into the empty shell case he was carrying. As they raced for cover with a Japanese fighter plane skimming the length of the debris-littered deck, cannon pumping away furiously, he cried above the racket, 'Die young and make a happy stiff, eh, Slack Arse. *Cheers!*'

Now the Japanese dive-bombers were swarming round the mighty British ship. They were like predatory birds, waiting to snatch a weak point in their prey's defences and strike. On the gundecks, the sweating, red-faced gunners worked all out. They knew just how vulnerable they were. The *Prince of Wales* was admittedly the most modern ship in the Royal Navy. All the same it had been designed to old standards, when surface ships expected to have to defend themselves against other major surface ships. The fact that in the future attacks would come in from the air and not from the sea had not been fully taken into account. Hence, the younger gunnery officers who knew this were determined to keep the Japanese planes with their armour-piercing bombs as well away from the *Wales* as possible.

So the marauding Mitsubishis met a solid wall, or so it seemed, of lethal steel every time they attempted to break through the defences and attack the great battleship's vulnerable superstructure. But these Japs were the bravest and most skilled in the Japanese Imperial Naval Air Force. They knew what was at stake; and they were not afraid of death. Time and time again they pressed home their advantage. Desperately, zig-zagging and twisting, they came in at sea level, cannon blazing, hands on toggles which would release their deadly eggs. It was a dream target for the gunners. At that range they could hardly miss. Concentrating on the planes with fat torpedoes tucked between their wheels, lowered to decrease their speed and give them a steadier platform for launching their deadly 'tin fish', the British gunners poured a merciless hail of fire at the Japanese.

The first plane was hit and exploded in a great ball of searing, angry red flame. One moment it was there; next moment it wasn't. Bits and pieces of shiny metal rained down, kicking up angry, furious spouts of water near the *Wales's* port bow.

The gunners cheered. Not for long. Yet another bold pilot was zooming down the length of the great ship's superstructure, looking for a weak spot in the barrage. The pilot didn't find one. For a few moments the sweating gunners could see him, a dark outline behind the gleaming perspex of his canopy, what looked like a white and red cloth* fluttering from his helmet. Then he was struck by the full blast of the massed 'Chicago pianos'. He seemed to melt away before their very eyes. The half-inch bullets ripped away the metal to reveal the spars beneath like the bones of some monstrous bird picked clean by some other predatory animal. With the pilot slumped across his shattered controls, dead, the plane slammed into the sea with a tremendous burst of water.

But the Japanese attackers were not to be denied. Again and again they came in, harrying and chasing and worrying the great ship like jackals attempting to bring down some wounded, magnificent beast of the jungle. A near miss exploded underwater. The *Wales* shuddered, as if struck a mighty blow by an invisible fist. She started to slow down immediately. Still her powerful engines throbbed on, but oil tinged the white fury of her wake now. The pilots saw

*The Rising Sun flag of Japan.

it. She had been hit in the engines or oil

300

storage tanks. They redoubled their efforts.

Now their tactics changed. They came in from all sides simultaneously. Coming in at wave-top height, their props thrashing the sea into a fury, they waited till they had almost crashed into the ship before launching their torpedoes.

The 'tin fish' with their two tons of high explosives were cleaving the water in all directions. Here and there desperate marksmen armed with tommy-guns and rifles, tried to pick them off. In vain. They were just beneath the water, their depth difficult to judge. But they were clearly there heading for the *Wales*, tracking through the sea, a flurry of air bubbles indicating their progress, in lethal, deadly-straight lines.

At last the inevitable happened. A sudden, ominous shudder. The great 35,000-ton ship heeled. Men were flung off their feet. An already drunken Big Slack Arse nearly dropped his bottle with the shock of the deadly impact. At his side Little Slack Arse reached out an urgent hand, crying above the murderous noise, 'What y're up ter, fart in a trance? I know it's gash*... But you–'

*Navy slang for 'free'.

The rest of his words werc drowned by a

301

weird creaking and groaning, as if there were some sorely troubled soul in the bowels of the ship making its protest at the misery it was being subjected to. Everything from top to bottom of the *Prince of Wales* shook and trembled. On the deck men grabbed stanchions and rails to support themselves. The wire hawsers of a lifeboat snapped. Like a giant whip the metal cable lashed across the deck. A rating went down screaming, his body torn in half, his severed legs thrashing in death agonies. The lifeboat went tumbling to the churned-up sea below.

The little admiral cried above the sudden alarm. 'Report ... report!'

A capless officer, face ashen, a trickle of bright red blood oozing down his ashen cheek came staggering onto the bridge. 'Two torpedoes ... sir,' he gasped, breath coming harshly as if from cracked leather bellows, 'Stern and ... hull ... First reports, the casings are ripped open...'

'Balls and bollocks!' the little admiral exploded. 'Not that–' he didn't finish his sentence. His trained eyes and ears told him they were already in trouble – serious trouble. The great ship was beginning to list to port and she was slowing down.

Next to him the harassed, bleeding officer

302

whispered aghast, as if he dared not express his thoughts aloud, 'The engineers are losing control already...'

They were. Steam was escaping everywhere down below. Engineer officers, trying to keep calm to impress the stokers, were stumbling and splashing their way through the turbines, their gleaming white overalls, soaked in seawater to the knees. Somewhere a CPO was calling in a thick Glaswegian accent, 'Dinna fash yersens, laddies... There's no need for panic, ye ken...'

Up at the control panel an engineer artificer, keen, professional and apparently calm, was viewing the various dials and panels, eyeing the oscillating red needles of the gauges and calling out his findings. 'Power going to steering ... ammunition hoists weakening...'

Indeed all the many sources of power and control which kept the great ship functioning and fighting back were beginning to go. Radar, radio, main anti-aircraft guns ... they were weakening by the instant, as the *Prince of Wales* tried valiantly, desperately, to fight off her attackers.

And the *Prince of Wales* was not alone. The *Repulse* was under severe attack too. All around, the destroyers tried to ward off the assault on the capital ships, but the *Repulse* had already been hit first and was losing speed rapidly. On his bridge, Captain Tennant, his battered peaked cap still cocked at its usual jaunty angle, was aghast at the sight. He had never thought in over a quarter of a century in the Royal Navy he'd ever see anything like this: two of His Majesty's greatest ships knocked virtually out of action, and in danger of sinking, by a handful of enemy planes. Suddenly it dawned upon him that he was the last of an old era. A new world was beginning to dawn. The great battleships with which he had grown up were finished.

But his bluff, square-chinned seadog's face revealed nothing of his questionings and uncertainties. If he and his ship had go under, they'd go under fighting with the dear old White Ensign flying bravely.

He looked through the smoke which was beginning to billow everywhere and at the deck littered with shell cases. There the bodies lay in the grotesque postures of those done violently to death. They were boys for the most part. Yet they had fought – and died – as bravely as the regulars. He swallowed momentarily and stared at the faces of the survivors, who continued to fight back, or simply waited, no more tasks to be done, for the inevitable. Their features reflected a mixture of incredulity and a sort of sensuous pleasure – he couldn't find another description for the look – but no fear. A officer with a bloodstained bandage around his head looked up and saw the captain staring at them. 'Plucky little buggers, the Japs, sir, aren't they? That was as beautiful attack as I ever expected to see...' Suddenly his legs faltered and folded beneath him like those of a new-born foal. He collapsed on the deck and died.

The end was near now. The destroyers were doing their best to protect the battleships. They circled them, firing all out like a circle of prairie wagons fighting off Red Indians. But the defensive firing was getting weaker by the minute, as more and more Japanese planes arrived to take up the fight. In the end there would be just short of a hundred of them, like a pack of savage hounds trying to pull down a grievously wounded buck at bay.

In those last minutes of the now one-sided fight, Tennant of the *Repulse* signalled Leach of the *Prince of Wales:* 'Have you sustained any serious damage?'

The pitiful answer came back almost at once through the thick, choking, black smoke which separated the two ships, 'We're out of control... Steering gear gone.'

Tennant sighed and tucked his cap straight. As an afterthought he did up the top buttons of his torn tunic. If he was going to die as a captain in the Royal Navy, he was going to do so tidily and dressed according to King's Regulations. He looked stern. Then he laughed at himself. Who would see him now? Besides, soon he'd be dead, just another of thousands, hundreds of thousands of British servicemen who would do their duty for 'King and Country', die, and be duly forgotten.

Somewhere through the racket – the thunder of the guns, the snarl and howl of attacking Japanese planes coming in for the kill now – he could hear the caterwauling of someone singing, '*And the mate at the wheel had a bloody good feel at the girl I left behind me... Ain't it a pity she's only one titty to feed the baby on, poor little bugger's only one udder...*' He laughed uproariously and shouted into the swirling fog of war that was submerging his sinking ship, 'That's the stuff to give the troops... Nil desp–'

On the *Prince of Wales* they were throwing

rafts, lifebelts, benches, bits of wood, anything that would float from the ship to the boiling sea below. A midshipman balanced on his toes, hands extended, on the top of the control tower of the main mast. He took a deep breath, controlling his breathing, as if he were competing in some Fleet diving championship before the war. Then he launched himself into space. He fell one hundred and seventy feet, cleaving the water in a perfect dive. Next instant he was up on the surface again and swimming powerfully to where – no one ever found out.

Others less skilled were diving from masts and control towers from the *Repulse* as well. The water was abruptly full of gasping, shouting men, their heads bobbing up and down in the waves. An old 'stripey' missed his distance and he slammed into the battle-cruiser's steel plates. Every bone in his body broke with a clearly audible sound. Next moment he tumbled into the sea like a sack of wet cement.

Tennant looked at the screws still churning away, driving the hundreds of men now in the water further from the sinking ship. He nodded his approval and said quietly, without any dramatics, 'You'd better get out of it now.'

The young officers who had assembled around him on the littered, tilting bridge looked at their skipper. 'Aren't you coming with us, sir?' two or three demanded eagerly.

The captain smiled again and shook his head gently. 'Off you go now. There's not much more time.'

'But, Captain,' a young lieutenant commander, digging his heels in as the bridge tilted even more, 'you must come with us. You've done all you can for the ship. More than most men could.'

Still hesitant the officers, who had already planned what to do if this happened, flashed a look at the lieutenant commander. He nodded. There was no more time to be lost. They grabbed him, dragged him to the side and without further ado flung him into the sea. Captain Tennant was saved...

No one attempted the same trick with that august commander of Force Z, Admiral Sir Thomas Phillips. He was last seen, standing at attention on the bridge of the *Prince of Wales* together with her skipper, Captain Leach. As the few remaining survivors jumped into the burning oil slick below, Leach was seen to wave and appeared to be saying, 'Goodbye... Good luck... God bless you.' Then the water rose up and covered them,

Not far away, a drunken old stripey – it might have been Big Slack Arse or his oppo, Little Slack Arse, who knows – was heard singing that cynical soldiers' song of that year so long ago ... *'Bless 'em all ... bless 'em all ... the long and the short and the tall ... you'll get no promotion this side of the ocean ... so cheer up my lads, bless 'em all...'*

Then, as the stern of the dying *Repulse* towered up above them like a church steeple, the water rose to meet him too, meeting and then covering him ... and all was silence.

Envoi

We are very sorry for what happened in that period. The Emperor has a responsibility to his country and to the world, so I believe he should apologize.

Eighteen-year-old Japanese, Yoko Yoshinari,
Cardiff, Wales, 27 May 1998

The Americans have forced upon us a one-sided view of history.

Japanese Historian Hideaki Kase,
Tokyo, Japan, 25 May 1998

'Bloody rotten Nips!' his mother exclaimed, eyeing the television fiercely, as if she might spring from her rocking chair and jump at it any moment, as she spooned down the pot noodles greedily – she had long given up her chopsticks. 'How can *our* Queen stand them. Everybody knows that all Nips stink.'

Professor 'Nobby' Chen-Clark sighed and laid down *The Times* he was reading. If his colleagues, Chinese and Japanese, at the School of Oriental Studies, could hear such sentiments, he'd be 'out on yer earhole, tootsweet', as his long-dead Dad would have said in that unmistakeable cockney accent of his. 'Now mother,' he said, speaking English.

His was flawless and hers, too, was very fluent, but she still couldn't really pronounce the 'r', making it sound like an 'l'. How often as a boy in short pants he had teased her with 'flied lice', until his father had croaked from the bed upon which he lay most of the time in the sitting room by then, 'One more 'flied lice' from you, Sonny Jim, and I'll give yer a clip around the lughole ... as sick as I am.'

Professor Chen-Clark smiled fondly at the memory. His cockney father had been very good really. He had coped with a Chinese 'missus' and 'a half-caste son' in a working-class estate, put him through grammar school and then, on his meagre wage at Smithfields, into university, though he had died before his 'half-caste' son had completed his first degree.

The Professor with the benign intelligent

face tried to concentrate on *The Times* report that he was attempting to read, while his mother glared at the royal procession, complete with the Emperor of Japan on his first state visit to Britain. Apparently, according to *The Times* correspondent, the latest Japanese twenty-million-dollar blockbuster, financed by a right-wing businessman, denied that the Imperial Japanese Army had ever committed atrocities during the war. As the correspondent wrote: 'It portrays Japan's invasion of Asian countries as a noble crusade to liberate them from European control... Moreover it credits Japan with a magnified role in freeing India from the yoke of British colonialism.'

The Professor, mild-mannered and even-tempered unlike his long-dead father, put *The Times* down with a little sigh. For such a high-tech nation, dependent on exports from abroad for its very existence, Japan remained a very closed society, insular, nationalistic, not wishing to hear the truth about its past, he told himself. There were excuses for this kind of attitude, he knew, but western peoples would never understand them. It was a question of 'face' really, he supposed, and looked across at his mother.

She was very old now and incredibly wrinkled. Yet, all the same, when she was angry she still had the fire of her youth in Malaya, which he guessed must have attracted his dear old Cockney dad to her in the first place.

'Look at the Duke,' his mother ranted, pointing a shaky, bony forefinger at the Duke of Edinburgh who was supporting himself with an umbrella – Chen-Clark told himself that the Duke was probably too vain to use a crutch. 'Now he's not bowing and scraping in front of the Nips.' She shook her head firmly. 'And shall I tell you why?'

He shook his head and said *sotto voce,* 'No, but all the same you *will*, Mother.'

He was right because she went on to say, 'Because he suffered at their hands, just like your dear old dad and that officer of his...' She clicked the fingers of her heavily beringed hand – like all Chinese she still believed in keeping her wealth on her body in the form of bracelets and rings – in irritation and cursed in Cantonese, 'God, I've forgotten his name again and I loved him once, nearly as much as your dead father.'

Tears flooded her rheumy eyes momentarily and he said hastily, trying to reassure her, 'It doesn't matter, Mother.'

'Oh yes it does,' she said pedantically, as on the screen, behind the lines of police and guardsmen present to shield the Imperial Japanese couple from the British crowd, the veterans turned their backs on their coach in a symbol of utter contempt. 'First you start forgettin' names, then you end forgetting *everything.*'

'As you say, Mother,' he said gently, trying to pacify her. 'I'll turn the telly off. It's upsetting you, dear.'

'Yes,' she answered weakly and he crossed the tiny sitting room, decorated with the brass ornaments and flying ducks which had been his father's choice for the 'best room'. He flicked the switch. The television went silent. Now the only sound was the harsh rasp of her breath coming through ruined lungs and that of one of the black kids next door revving up his motorbike while he adjusted his dreadlocks wig under the big floppy knitted cap.

For a few moments in the new silence, Professor Chen-Clark thought of that day of which he had read so much: that February day when that 'buck-teethed git', as his father had always called General Percival, had surrendered Singapore to the victorious

Japanese. It had really symbolized the end of the British Empire. Though no one had known it that terrible afternoon, with the dead being savaged by hungry dogs on the streets of the shell-battered island, the British had lost India in a matter of hours. The rest of the Empire on which the sun never set, had gone over the next ten years.

With it had gone the hopes and pride of people like his dead father, who had been as much victim of the Japanese conquerors as if they had bayonetted him on the spot as they had done his defiant CO, Major Nairs. Those three dreadful years in the camps had killed him in the end.

'Don't get upset, mother,' he said, hastily coming out of his reverie. He knew the signs. Her hands were trembling so violently she had been forced to drop her favourite pot noodles, scattering them over the 'best' carpet like the white worms his father had been forced to eat in the camps to survive. The side of her wizened old face was puckering up. It was the start of the tears which always flowed at these times, now that she was staring at the picture of her husband and Major Nairs, dressed in absurdly long khaki shorts and great solar topees, carrying out the 'white man's

315

burden' somewhere or other, no doubt. 'It's all a long time ago now.'

The tears vanished as swiftly as they had come. She swung round on him with surprising speed for such an old, sick woman. Her eyes blazed with fury and anger – he couldn't describe them otherwise. 'What do you know, *boy*!' she spat at him venomously.

The 'boy' hurt. Here he was a fifty-year-old respected professor of Oriental Studies at one of the world's greatest universities, and she, the daughter of a Chinese village storekeeper-cum-moneylender, was treating him like some ignorant coolie. 'You mustn't speak to me like that–'

'Hold your mouth,' she interrupted him fiercely. 'You think – all of your generation do – because you are clever and have many degrees that you know everything. You think that we are silly old people, who would be better off dead, always living in the past like we do.'

'Mother,' he commenced, trying to pacify her. 'You know what the doctor said–'

'I shit on the sawbones!' she shrieked, literally translating from Cantonese into English. 'He knows nothing either – with his fat gut.' She poked a bony forefinger at him.

'Indian bastard!'

If she hadn't been his own mother, he would have laughed at this enraged old woman, with her blazing eyes and flushed, furious face. How xenophobic she was! And she had not even been born in England.

'You know nothing. Nothing about us. Nothing about the pride we once felt. Nothing about how we suffered. Nothing about how we kept our mouths shut all those years. Nothing about how we resented you, living like fat pigs in shit – in ... in ... *your shitting Welfare State!*' she spat out the name, as if it were the epitome of everything that was disgusting.

'I'll get you a nice drink of gin,' he volunteered, knowing how she dearly loved her favourite tipple, even if it was still morning. 'That'll soothe you down a bit, Mother.' He rose to his feet.

She looked at him, skinny chest breathing hard, as if she had just run a great race. Her old eyes no longer blazed with rage. Instead that look had been replaced with one of contempt, even cynicism. Now she spoke in a whisper, as if to herself so that he had to strain to hear her, trying to cut out the noise from the 'ghetto-blaster' next door. 'The day those two ships went down, we knew

317

that it was the end ... it was all over ... that there was no hope for us any more...' She broke off suddenly and bent her old grey head.

He stared down at his mother's head, bottle of Gordon's Gin in his hand, totally confused. 'Ships?' Professor Chen-Clark whispered to himself. *What ships...?*

The publishers hope that this book has given you enjoyable reading. Large Print Books are especially designed to be as easy to see and hold as possible. If you wish a complete list of our books please ask at your local library or write directly to:

Magna Large Print Books
Magna House, Long Preston,
Skipton, North Yorkshire.
BD23 4ND

This Large Print Book for the partially sighted, who cannot read normal print, is published under the auspices of

THE ULVERSCROFT FOUNDATION